THE MASK

A Story of Love and Adventure

ARTHUR HORNBLOW

1st WORLD
LIBRARY
Literary Society

The Mask

Arthur Hornblow

© 1st World Library, 2006
PO Box 2211
Fairfield, IA 52556
www.1stworldlibrary.com
First Edition

LCCN: 2007920621

Softcover ISBN: 978-1-4218-3929-5
Hardcover ISBN: 978-1-4218-3829-8
eBook ISBN: 978-1-4218-4029-1

Purchase *"The Mask"*
as a traditional bound book at:
www.1stWorldLibrary.com/purchase.asp?ISBN=978-1-4218-3929-5

1st World Library is a literary, educational organization
dedicated to:

- Creating a free internet library of downloadable ebooks

- Hosting writing competitions and offering book
publishing scholarships.

Interested in more 1st World Library books?
contact: literacy@1stworldlibrary.com
Check us out at: www.1stworldlibrary.com

1st World Library Literary Society

Giving Back to the World

"If you want to work on the core problem, it's early school literacy."

- James Barksdale, former CEO of Netscape

"No skill is more crucial to the future of a child, or to a democratic and prosperous society, than literacy."

- Los Angeles Times

Literacy... means far more than learning how to read and write... The aim is to transmit... knowledge and promote social participation."

- UNESCO

"Literacy is not a luxury, it is a right and a responsibility. If our world is to meet the challenges of the twenty-first century we must harness the energy and creativity of all our citizens."

- President Bill Clinton

"Parents should be encouraged to read to their children, and teachers should be equipped with all available techniques for teaching literacy, so the varying needs and capacities of individual kids can be taken into account."

- Hugh Mackay

CHAPTER I

"There! What did I tell you? The news is out!"

With a muttered exclamation of annoyance, Kenneth Traynor put down his coffee cup with a crash and, leaning over the table, pointed out to his wife a despatch from London, given prominence in the morning paper, which ran as follows:

Advices from Cape Town report the finding on a farm near Fontein, a hundred miles north of here, of a diamond which in size is only second to the famous Koh-i-noor. The stone, which is in the shape of an egg with the top cut off, weighs 1,649 carats, and was discovered after blasting at the foot of some rocks on land adjacent to the tract owned by the Americo-African Mining Company of New York. It is understood that the American Company is negotiating for the property; some say the transfer has already been made. If this is true, the finding of this colossal stone means a windfall for the Yankee stockholders.

The Traynor home, No.—Gramercy Park, was one of those dignified, old-fashioned residences that still remain in New York to remind our vulgar, ostentatious *nouveaux riches* of the days when culture and refinement counted for something more than mere wealth. Overlooking the railed-in square with its green lawns, pretty winding paths and well-dressed children romping at play, it had a high stoop which opened into a wide hall, decorated with obsolete weapons and trophies of the hunt. On the right were rich tapestries, masking the folding doors of a spacious drawing-room, richly decorated and furnished in Louis XIV. period. Beyond this, to the rear of the house which had been built out to the extreme end of the lot, was the splendidly appointed dining-room with its magnificent fireplace of sculptured white marble, surmounted by a striking portrait in oils by Carolus Duran of Mrs. Traynor—a painting which had been one of the most successful pictures of the previous year's salon.

In a clinging, white silk negligee gown, the gossamer folds of which only partially veiled the outlines of a slender, graceful figure, Helen sat at the breakfast table opposite her husband, toying languidly with her knife and fork. It was nearly noon, long past the usual breakfast time, and by every known gastronomical law her appetite should have been on keen edge. But this morning she left everything untasted. Even the delicious wheat cakes, which none better than Mammy, their Southern cook, knew how to do to a point, did not tempt her. They had been out to dinner the night before. Her head ached; she was nervous and feverish. Always full of good spirits and laughter, ever the soul and life of the house, it was unusual to find her in this mood, and if her husband, now voraciously devouring the tempting array of ham and eggs spread before him, had not been so absorbed in the news of the day, he would have quickly noticed it, and guessed there was something amiss.

Certainly the appearance of the dining-room was enough to upset the nerves of anyone, especially a sensitive young woman who prided herself on her housekeeping. All around was chaos and confusion. The usually sedate, orderly dining-room was littered with trunks, grips, umbrellas and canes enveloped in rugs—all the confusion incidental to a hurried departure.

She took the newspaper, read the despatch and handed it back in silence.

"Isn't that the very deuce!" he went on peevishly. "We've been trying our utmost to keep it secret. Unless we're quick, there'll be a rush of adventurers from all parts of the world before we can secure the options. Happily the despatch is vague. They don't know all the facts. If they did—" Lowering his voice and looking around cautiously to make sure that the butler had left the room and no one was listening, he continued: "Besides you know what I am to bring back. It couldn't be entrusted to anyone else. Just think—a stone worth nearly a million dollars! I hope no one will guess I have it in my possession. It must be brought safe to New York. That's why it's so important that I go at once. Even by catching the *Mauretania* to-morrow, I can't reach Cape Town for a month, and every moment counts now."

As Helen was still silent he glanced across the table at her for the first time. Her pallor and the drooping lines about her mouth told him something was wrong. Instantly concerned, he asked:

"What's the matter, dear?"

"I'm horribly nervous."

"What about?"

"This trip of yours, of course."

"You ought to be used to them by this time. This isn't the first time I've had to leave you since our marriage."

"I didn't mind the other trips so much. When you went to Mexico and Alaska, it didn't seem so far away. But this journey to South Africa is different. You are running a terrible risk carrying that diamond. I can't shake off a horrible feeling that something dreadful will happen."

Surprised less at what she said than at her serious manner, he laid down the newspaper, and, jumping up, went over to her. His wife sat motionless, her lips trembling, her large eyes filled with tears. In spite of a palpable effort at self-control, it was evident that she was laboring under great nervous tension. Bending caressingly over her, he said anxiously:

"Why Helen, old girl! What's the matter?"

She made no answer. Her head fell on his breast. For a moment she could not speak. Her emotion seemed to choke her utterance, paralyze her speech. He insisted:

"What is it, dearie?" he demanded.

"I'm so nervous about your going, I'm so afraid about your having the diamond," she sobbed. Suddenly, as if unable longer to control herself, she rose from the table and threw her arms around his neck. Passionately she cried: "Oh, Kenneth, don't go! Don't go! I feel that something will happen."

He laughed carelessly as he fondled her. More seriously he replied:

"I hope something does happen. That's what I'm going out there for. Why, Helen dear, I don't think you quite realize what this trip means to us. If the deal goes through, and we get full control of all that property, we'll all be as rich as Croesus. Just think, dear, 300,000 square miles of the most wonderful diamond producing country. In ten days they found 400 beautifully clear stones, some of them weighing over a hundred carats. If the reports are true, we shall have a group of mines as valuable as the famous De Beers group. Do you know what they have produced to date in actual money?"

The young woman shook her head. Usually she was glad enough to listen to her husband's business plans, but to-day they wearied her. Her mind was too much preoccupied with something that concerned her far more. The idea of this coming separation, the knowledge that he was running a risk, had left her singularly depressed. She had tried to remain calm and control her emotion, but the effort was beyond her. The prospect of this separation, with its vague, undefined forebodings of disaster, was simply intolerable. The tears she was unable to restrain rolled silently down her cheeks.

He looked at her in surprise. Never had he seen her in this mood. Approaching her more closely, he said kindly:

"That can't be the only reason, dear, what's the matter?"

She hesitated a moment before she answered:

"I'm very nervous to-day. I was dreadfully irritated last night at the dinner. I wish I hadn't gone—"

"Who irritated you?"

"That man Signor Keralio. I simply can't tolerate the man. How I hate him!"

"Why—what did he do?"

"He did nothing. He wouldn't dare—there. But I wouldn't care to be alone with him. His eyes were enough. He imagines he is irresistible, and that every woman is immoral. That is the kind of man he is. He annoyed me all evening. There was no getting away from him."

Kenneth laughed and went back to finish his breakfast, quite indifferent to what he had just heard. He knew his wife too well to be afraid of any number of Signor Keralios. Humming a tune, he said carelessly:

"Why didn't you call me?"

"What? Create a scandal? That would only make me ridiculous. He wouldn't care. I can't bear the sight of the man, yet I have to be polite to him."

Kenneth nodded.

"Yes—I have reasons for not caring to quarrel with Keralio just now."

She looked up quickly.

"Why? What is that man to you? He's your fencing master, I know, but that's no reason for making a friend of him. I never understood why you associated with him. He is so different to you."

Her husband smiled. He adored his wife and admired the sex in general, but, like most men, he had never had much respect for women's judgment. Women were made to be loved; not to discuss business with. Indulgently he said:

"My dear, you don't understand. I have important financial relations with Keralio. I don't care for him myself, but one can't choose one's business associates. He and I are interested in a silver mine in Mexico. Thanks to him, I got in on the ground floor. One of these days the investment will bring me a big return."

His wife shrugged her shoulders. Incredulously she retorted:

"Not if Keralio has anything to do with it. I don't trust him. He has deceit and evil written all over his face."

Amused at her petulance, Kenneth jumped up impulsively and took his wife in his arms.

Abandoning herself willingly to his embrace, for a moment her head fell back on his broad shoulder, and she smiled up at him. From her soft, yielding form arose that subtle, familiar perfume, the intoxicating, vague, indefinable aroma of the well groomed woman that never fails to set a man's blood on fire. Bending low until his mouth touched hers, he kissed her until her face glowed under the ardor of his amative caress. But to-day she was not in the mood to respond.

"Don't—don't!" she panted, striving to free herself.

"Admit that you're foolish or I'll do it again," he laughed.

"Perhaps I am. It's selfish of me to make it harder for you to go away."

The butler reentered the room with the finger bowls, and she quickly disengaged herself. To hide her confusion, she turned to the servant:

"Did my sister go out, Robert?"

"Yes, m'm," replied the man respectfully. "Miss Ray told me to tell you in case you asked that she had gone shopping and would be back soon."

"Where's Miss Dorothy?"

"The fraulein took her to the park, m'm."

"When fraulein comes in, tell her to bring Dorothy upstairs."

"Very well, m'm."

The butler went out and Helen turned to her husband. Anxiously she said:

"I've been a little worried about Dorothy lately. She's not looking well. I think she needs the country."

Kenneth looked up quickly. Next to his wife he loved his flaxen haired little girl better than anything in the world. There was a worried look on his face as he asked:

"What does the doctor say?"

"Oh, it's nothing to be alarmed at. Only she's growing fast, and needs all the air possible. I'm thinking of sending her to

Aunt Carrie for a while. You know she has a beautiful place in the suburbs of Philadelphia. She would be out in the air all the time."

"Yes—that's a good idea. Send her there by all means. Write your aunt to-night."

Helen glanced at the clock. There wasn't any time to lose. Turning to her husband she said quickly:

"You had better come upstairs and finish your packing, dear. Your trunks aren't nearly ready and the expressman was ordered for three."

Recalled thus abruptly to the day's duties, he turned docily and followed her upstairs.

Beautiful as was the Traynor home below, it was in the library in the second floor that Helen always felt happiest and most at ease. Up the broad, thickly carpeted stairs and turning to the right as the landing was reached, they entered the library, a room of truly noble proportions extending the entire width of the house and with deep recessed windows and low seats, overlooking the park. The furnishings, though simple, were rich and luxurious. The woodwork was of black Flemish oak, the ceiling beamed with a dull red background. The upholstery was a rich red plush throughout, with deep seated armchairs, and sofas built close to the wall wherever space permitted. In the corners, numerous electric reading lamps could be turned on or off at pleasure, constituting ideal nooks for reading. The furniture, apart from the red plush armchairs, was of black Flemish oak to match the woodwork, with an immense richly carved black oak dark table in the center of the room, lighted by an electrolier of similar size and design to the one in the dining-room.

It was in this room with its atmosphere of books so conducive to peace and introspection that Helen loved to spend her spare time. The walls were literally lined with tomes, dealing with every branch of human knowledge—religion, science, philosophy, literature. Here when alone she enjoyed many an intellectual treat, browsing among the world's treasures of the mind. Even when her sister had a few intimates to tea, or when friends dropped in in the evening, they always preferred being in the library to anywhere else.

Only second to the library in the affection of its young mistress was her bed chamber with which it was connected by a small boudoir. Furnished in Louis XVI. style, it was a beautiful room, decorated in the most dainty and delicate of tones. The bed, copied after Marie Antoinette's couch in the Little Trianon was in sculptured Circassian walnut, upholstered in dull pink brocade, the broad canopy overhead being upheld by two flying cupids. The handsome dressing table with three mirrors and chairs were of the same wood and period. On the floor was a thick carpet especially woven to match the other furnishings.

To-day, littered as it was with trunks and clothes, the room lacked its usual sedateness and dignity, but Helen did not mind. She would have preferred it to look far worse if only her loved one were not going away. His clothes lay scattered all over the floor. There was still much to be done.

Kenneth himself realized it as he ruefully surveyed the scene. Hurry he must. A director's meeting to-night, the steamer sailing to-morrow and here he was not nearly ready. Helen could see no reason why Francois should not do the packing, but he insisted on doing it himself, and was soon deep in the work of filling the trunks that stood around.

While he worked, almost unconscious of her presence, she sat disconsolately on a trunk and watched him, and from time to time, as if ashamed to let him see her weakness, she turned her head aside to furtively wipe away a tear. No doubt her misgivings were foolish. Husbands left their wives on business trips every day. Sensible women were not so silly as to cry over it. It was to be only temporary, she knew that, yet her heart misgave her. She had tried to be resigned to this South African journey, to accept it without protest, but her feelings were too much for her. When she married Kenneth Traynor, the energetic, prosperous Wall Street promoter, everybody knew that it was a love match. Standing six feet two in his stockings, muscular, sinewy, without an ounce of superfluous fat, Kenneth Traynor looked as though he could give a good account of himself no matter in what tight place he found himself. His clean cut features and strong chin denoted strength of character, his deep set blue eyes, a blue of a shade so light rarely seen except in the peasants of Normandy, beamed with frankness and honesty, a kindly smile hovered about his smooth, firm mouth. What at once attracted attention was his hair which was dark and unusually thick and bushy and a peculiar characteristic was a solitary white lock in the center of his forehead. Such a phenomenon of the capillary glands was not uncommon, but as a rule, the white hair is on the side of or at the back of the head. In Kenneth's case, it was the very center of the forehead and imparted to his face an individuality quite its own.

When on leaving college, he had been forced, like other young men, to choose a career, he was unable to decide what he wanted to do. Doctor, lawyer, architect, author—none of these suited his nervous, restless temperament. He craved a more exciting life, and at one time thought seriously of entering the army with the hope of seeing active service in the Philippines. But Aguinaldo's surrender put a quietus on this project, and he entered a broker's office in Wall Street Here, in the maelstrom of frenzied finance, his pent up energies found an outlet. He went into the stock gambling game with the feverish energy of a born gambler. Months of excitement followed, luck being usually with him. He was successful. He doubled and tripled his capital, after which he had good sense enough to stop, withdrawing from the fray before the tide turned. But he could not give up the life entirely. The business of stock promotion was the next best substitute. It was about that time he met the woman he married.

It had been an ideal union in every way, but even Helen herself could not have guessed that day now three years ago when she left the church a bride, how completely, how entirely this man whose sterling qualities, good nature and charm of manner had won her heart, would take complete possession of her, body and soul. Instead of the romance flickering out after the first sudden blaze of fierce passion, as it usually does after the first few months of married life, on her side, at least, the flame had gathered in strength until now it was the one compelling, all absorbing interest in her life.

She recalled how they had first met. It was in the Winter time. She was skating in Central Park. A thaw had set in and the ice was dangerous. Suddenly there was an ominous crack, and the crowd scurried out of harm's way, all but one child, a little nine year old girl who, in her eagerness to escape, stumbled and fell. The next instant she was in the water, disappearing under the ice. Just at that moment, a tall athletic figure dashed swiftly to the hole and, stooping quickly, caught the child by the dress. Then, by a feat of almost superhuman strength which awed the crowd into silence, he drew the little victim out to safety, not much the worse for her experience.

Spellbound, hardly able to breathe from sheer excitement, Helen had watched the work of rescue. When the stranger, tall, muscular, handsome, passed her, carrying tenderly his burden, a human life saved from a watery grave, she could not help murmuring:

"Oh, how brave of you!"

"Nonsense," he retorted abruptly. "It's nothing to make a fuss about."

She did not see him again for six months, and had almost forgotten the incident when one night at the opera during a performance of "Tannhauser," a man, tall, square shouldered, entered the box where she was and was presented to her.

"Helen—Mr. Traynor."

It was her hero.

He had remained her hero ever since.

She remembered the afternoon when he had asked her to be his wife. They were alone in the library which overlooked the Park with its beautiful vista of green foliage, its glimpse of rolling lawns, and shimmering lakes. They were standing side by side, gazing idly out of the window, conversing quietly on all kinds of topics interesting to them both. She was enjoying his vigorous, masculine point of view and feeling strangely happy in his company.

"When should a man marry?" he asked all at once.

Startled for a moment at the abruptness of the question which nothing in their previous conversation had led up to, she answered gravely:

"When he's tired of being alone and when he feels he has met the woman with whom he can be happy, the kind of woman who will be a real helpmate and aid him to achieve his ambitions."

"How can he know that the woman to whom he is attracted will have this influence in his life? How can he distinguish real gold from the imitation which merely glitters?"

"Only by his instinct. That never errs."

"And when in your opinion, should a woman marry?"

"When she meets the man to whom she feels she can give herself without forfeiting her self-respect."

He nodded approvingly, and looked at her for a few moments without speaking. Outside it was growing dark, for which she

Arthur Hornblow

was glad, for her face burned under the earnestness of his gaze. Finally he said:

"You are right. But yours is a point of view the modern girl seldom takes. First she discusses ways and means. Love, self respect—these she considers quite negligible."

She protested.

"Not all girls—only some girls. They are foolish virgins who leave their lamps untrimmed. They sow folly to-day only to reap unhappiness to-morrow."

He said nothing and for a few moments they both stood there in the increasing darkness. Suddenly, without a moment's warning, his voice broken by emotion, he turned to her and said:

"I am tired of being alone. I have met the woman with whom I could be happy, the woman who can help me to do big things. Helen, I want you to be my wife."

She made no answer. She felt herself growing pale. A strange tremor passed through her entire body.

He came closer and took her unresisting hand.

"Helen," he whispered, "I want you for my wife."

Still no reply, but her small delicate hand remained clasped in his big, strong one, and gradually he drew her toward him until she was so close in his embrace that he could feel her panting breath on his cheek.

A strange thrill passed through him as he came in contact with her soft, yielding body. She never wore corsets, preferring the clinging Grecian style of gowns that showed graceful lines and left the figure free, and her form, slender yet firm and delicately chiseled like that of some sculptured goddess, had none of that voluptuous grossness which mars the symmetry of many women, otherwise beautiful.

As she nestled there, pale and trembling in his strong arms, he did not dare move, for fear that he might unwittingly injure a being so frail and delicate. All his life Kenneth had lived a clean life. He had not led the riotous, licentious kind of existence which some men of his means and opportunities think necessary to their comfort. He had never been a libertine. He had respected women; indeed, had rather avoided them.

But if a man, busily engaged in the battle of life, his mind always engrossed in serious affairs, succeeds in keeping natural instincts under control there comes a day when nature asserts herself, when his manhood demands the satisfaction of legitimate cravings. This bachelor who had lived a secluded, hermit-like kind of existence till he was thirty was suddenly and violently awakened to the fact that he was made of flesh and blood as are other men. This slim girl with her sweet ways, her pretty face, her ready wit, had completely vanquished him, and not alone did she satisfy him mentally, she also attracted him physically.

He realized it now as he held her tight against his breast. Her head had fallen on his shoulder. Her face with its pale, delicate profile was turned toward him, the eyes half closed. The mouth, arched like Cupid's bow and partly open, disclosing the white, moistened teeth, and red and luscious like some rare exotic fruit, was tempting enough to madden a saint. Kenneth was only human. Unable to resist, he lowered his head until his mouth grazed hers and then with a wild, almost savage exclamation of joy, the exultant cry of lust awakened and gratified, his lips met hers and lingered.

To Helen it seemed as though she was in a dream of untold ecstasy. Always a shrinking, modest girl, especially in the company of the opposite sex, in any calmer moment she would have been shocked beyond expression at this momentary abandonment she permitted herself. As she lay in this man's arms and felt his warm kisses on her lips, there came over her a strange sensation she had never known before. She grew dizzy and for a moment thought she would faint. All at once he released her. Almost apologetically, he murmured:

"Forgive me—I lost control over myself—I want you Helen— I want you for my wife. Will you marry me?"

She drew away and turned away her head, so he might not see her burning cheeks.

He persisted.

"Will you marry me?"

She hesitated a moment before replying. Then, very simply, she answered:

"Yes, Kenneth."

That was three years ago.

CHAPTER II

In a certain set Helen Traynor was not popular. Some people thought her old fashioned, strait-laced, prudish. They resented her having no taste for their frivolous, decadent amusements. They called her proud and condescending whereas, as a matter of fact, she merely asked to be let alone. Of course, it was only people whose opinions were worthless that criticized her. All who were admitted to her intimacy knew that there was no friend more loyal, no woman more womanly and charming.

In one respect she might be called old fashioned. Her views on life had certainly little in common with those held by most present-day women. She had no taste for bridge, she refused to adopt freak fashions in dress, she discouraged the looseness of tone in speech and manner so much affected by other women of her acquaintance—in a word she was in society but not of it. Naturally, she had more acquaintances than friends, yet she was not unpopular among her intimates. While secretly they laughed at what they termed her puritanical notions, they were shrewd enough to realize that they could hardly afford to snub a woman whose husband occupied so prominent a position in the world of affairs. Besides, was it not to their interest to cultivate her? Who gave more delightful dinners, who could on occasion be a more charming hostess? An accomplished musician, a clever talker, she easily dominated in whatever salon she happened to be, and the men were always found crowding eagerly around her.

Like most women of her temperament, sure of themselves and

in whose mind never enters even a thought of disloyalty to her marriage vows, she made no concealment of her preference for the masculine sex. With those men who were attracted by her unusual mentality,—she was gracious, and affable, discussing with politicians, jurists, financiers, economic and sociological questions with a brilliancy and insight that fairly astonished them. With literary men and musicians, she chatted intelligently of the latest novels and pictures and operas with the facility and expertness of a connoisseur. Other men, drawn by her exceptional beauty, fascinated by the spell of her soulful eyes, her tall graceful figure, and delicate classic face, framed in Grecian head dress, made violent love to her, their heated imaginations and jaded senses conceiving a conquest compared with which the criminal passion of Paolo for Francesca should pale. These would-be Lotharios might as well have tried to set an iceberg on fire. Quietly, but firmly and in unmistakable terms, she let them understand that they were wasting their time and their ardor thus quenched, one by one they dropped away and left her in peace. Only Signor Keralio had persisted. She had snubbed him, insulted him, time after time, yet wherever she turned she found him at her elbow. Society soon resigned itself to considering her as one apart—a beautiful, chaste Juno whose ideals all must respect. Indeed, the only thing with which she could be reproached was that she was in love with her husband—the unpardonable sin in society's eyes—but seeing who it was and despairing of ever changing her point of view, society forgave her.

It never occurred to Helen that she was different in any way from other women. She did not see how it was possible for a woman to be untrue to the man whose name she bore and still retain her self-respect. The day she ceased to love her husband she would leave him forever. To her way of thinking, it was shocking to go on living with a man merely because it suited one's convenience and comfort. She knew married women who did not care for their husbands, some actually detested the men they had married, and had always held in horror the intimate relation which marriage sanctioned. She felt sorry for such women, but secretly she despised them. They alone were to blame. Had they not married knowing well that there was no real affection in their hearts for the men to whom they gave themselves? The cynicism and effrontery of young girls regarding marriage particularly revolted her. Eager for wealth and social position, they offered themselves with brazen effrontery in the matrimonial market, immodestly displaying their charms to the lecherous, covetous eyes of blase, degenerate men. Any question of attachment, love, affection was never for a moment considered. The idea that a man could be even considered unless he were able to provide a fine establishment was laughed to scorn. The girls were all men hunters but they hunted only rich men. They called the feeling they experienced for the man they caught in their toils "love." They meant something quite different. To a girl of Helen's ideas, such manoeuvers were shocking. To her the marriage tie was something sacred, a relation not to be entered into lightly. Kenneth was rich, it was true, but she would have loved him none the less had he been one of his own fifteen dollar a week clerks. When they were married and the romance was over, he stopped playing the lover to devote himself to the more serious business of making money, but with her, time, instead of dimming the flame, only caused it to burn the brighter. This man whom she had married was her only thought. In him centered every interest of her life.

A muffled outburst of profanity from Kenneth aroused her from her reveries.

"That's always the way when one's in a hurry," he exclaimed petulantly. "Ring for Francois. Why the devil isn't he here?"

Quickly, Helen sprang up from the trunk and touched an electric button.

"What's the matter, dear?" she asked.

She approached her husband who, at the far end of the room, was red in the face from the unusual exertion of trying to coax the buckle of a strap into a hole obviously out of reach. He pulled and strained till the muscles stood out on his neck and brawny arms like whipcord, and still the obstinate buckle declined to be coerced. The more it resisted, the more determined he was to make it obey. Go in it must, if sheer strength would do it. The vice-president of the Americo-African Mining Company was no weakling. A six-foot athlete and captain of the Varsity football team in his college days, his muscles had been toughened in a thousand lively scrimmages and in later life plenty of golf, rowing and other out-of-door sports had kept him in condition. When he pulled hard something had to give way. It did in this instance. There was a tearing, rending sound and the strap broke off short. With a gesture of despair he turned to his wife as men are wont to do when in trouble.

"Wouldn't that jar you?" he cried, as he threw the broken strap away. "What the deuce am I going to do now?"

"Why don't you let Francois attend to such things?" answered his wife calmly. "He understands packing so much better than you. You're so strong, you break everything."

She looked fondly at her husband's tall, athletic figure. He turned to her with a smile.

"I guess you're right," he said. "But where the devil is Francois?"

"I don't know. I sent him downstairs to tell the cook to have some nice sandwiches ready when you come home after the director's meeting tonight, but that's an hour ago—"

His ill humor gone, Kenneth looked up and smiled at her. Putting his arm about her, fondly he said:

"Dear little wife. You're always thinking of the comfort of others. You're the most unselfish, the most adorable, the most—"

"Stop, Kenneth, don't be foolish or I shall believe you—"

His face red from his recent exertions, he sat down on the arm of a chair to rest a little. Full of the coming journey, he had already forgotten his wife's anxiety. The great business schemes he had in mind dwarfed for the time being every other consideration. He could think and talk of nothing but diamonds. Huge crystals, worth untold millions as big as a fist, flashed at him from every corner of the room. Fabulous fortunes had been made in the diamond mines of South Africa. Why should he not be as successful as others? The romance of the Cullinan might be repeated, even surpassed. Well he recalled how he had been thrilled by the sensational story of the discovery of that colossal gem, more than three times the size of the Excelsior, the wonder of the modern world. In imagination, he saw it now. An old-fashioned Boer farm, transformed into a modern mining camp. A moonlight night. A man strolling idly along the rugged, desolate veldt, chances to look down. His eye suddenly catches a gleam in the rough face of the jagged slope. He stoops and picks up what looks like a piece of ice. Quickly he returns to his office and hands it to his chief. The men look at each other in silence. To all parts of the world goes the message that a diamond has been found four times bigger than the largest gem in the world. A stone weighing over 3,000 carats and worth four million dollars. He could already imagine himself far from civilization among the barren mountains of South Africa, prospecting in wide stretches of stone and gravel, picking up the brilliant dazzling stones by the handful.

"Have you any idea," he said, "what the mines have produced?"

She shook her head indifferently.

"No, and I don't want to know. I don't want you to go—that's all."

"Their output in the last ten years is estimated at no less than

$400,000,000. Just think of it. Four hundred millions! Well, dear, I and a few others want some of it, and we're going to get it."

"But aren't we rich enough already?" she demanded petulantly. "Why this fever to get richer and richer? We are happy with what we have. Why run the risks to gain what after all will only be a surplus? We can't possibly spend it."

Her husband's eyes flashed. The lines about his mouth tightened as he retorted:

"One never has enough! You women don't understand. As long as you have all the amusement you crave, all the frocks you want, all the jewelry you covet, you think that is all there is to life."

She looked up at him reproachfully and seemed about to protest when he added hurriedly:

"Oh, I don't mean you. I know you are not that kind of woman. You are more serious, more sensible. I mean the average society woman whose only concern in life is dress and show. We men have different aims, higher ambitions. I'm well to do, as the term goes. I have an income of over $100,000 a year, a splendidly appointed town house, a show place in the country. Above all I have the most adorable wife in all the world. Most men would be satisfied. I am not. I want still more. I have the money craze, an uncontrollable lust to pile up millions. My ambition is to wield the power that only the possession of vast wealth confers. The resources of this vast country are practically in the hands of half a dozen men. Merely by holding up a finger, these men could, to suit their own selfish ends, start a universal panic which might bring about a financial cataclysm, involving the whole world in disaster. I do not say they would use this power for evil, but they are in position to do so if it served their purpose. I want to have such power, only if I had it I would not use it for evil. I would use it for good. Conditions in the industrial world are very critical. We are rapidly approaching a crisis. In all countries the forces of labor and the forces of capital are lined up in silent, grim battalions. The poor are getting poorer; the rich are getting richer. The cost of living is going up beyond all reason. Why? Because the men who control the wealth of the world will it so. The system which is responsible for this must one day, sooner or later, give way to another and more humane system, still to be devised, which will enable the man who produces the wealth of the world at least to enjoy some of the fruits of his toil. Now it goes into the hands of the privileged few who use the power their money gives them to keep their less fortunate fellow men in servile subjection. I want to be rich, very rich, but I will use my wealth for good. With it I will help my fellow man rise from the mire. I will help him throw off the shackles with which conscienceless capitalism has fettered him. I want to be such a power for good. I want—"

The maid reentered the room.

"Francois is not in his room, m'm."

Kenneth gave vent to an exclamation of impatience. Turning to his wife, he asked:

"Where is he? Did you send him anywhere?"

Helen shook her head. Quickly she said:

"He's never around except when he's not wanted."

It was so seldom that his wife displayed irritation at any one that Kenneth looked up in surprise.

"He's shopping, too, I suppose. You know there's little time left and he has things to get ready the same as I have."

Helen made a gesture of disapproval. Quickly she said:

"I wish you were going with someone else, with anyone but that man. I never liked him."

Her husband laughed. Carelessly he replied:

"I know you never did and it's the only instance since we're married where I've found dear little wife to be absolutely unfair. Seriously, sweetheart, your baseless prejudice against Francois is unworthy of you. I can't go without a servant of some kind. He's an honest fellow and a faithful servant."

Helen shrugged her shoulders.

"I'm not so sure about that," she retorted quickly. "What do you know about him or his honesty? He's a perfect stranger that blew in three months ago from nowhere. He had written recommendations which may be forged. You never took the trouble to look them up."

"Yes, I did. I asked Keralio about him."

Helen looked up in surprise.

"Signor Keralio? I didn't know Francois was ever with him."

"He was with him nearly a year. Keralio warmly recommends him and says he is a very faithful fellow. He only left him because he objected to being compelled to practise sword-play with his master. One day Keralio's foil slipped. Francois got a puncture and it made him nervous."

"No wonder I don't like him. Like master, like valet—as the French say."

Her husband smiled.

"You are down on Keralio, aren't you?"

"I detest him. How could any self-respecting woman like such a man? His every glance is an insult. With his polished manners and sardonic smile he reminds one of Mephistopheles."

"I don't fancy the fellow much myself, but I have to be polite to him. As I told you, he's in with the people who own that silver mine. I've found him useful."

"Don't trust him," replied Helen warningly. "If he makes himself useful to you, depend upon it, he has some ulterior motive in view. Now I know Francois was once with him I shall dislike him more than ever."

"Come—come dear," protested Kenneth, "that is carrying things too far. Francois is quite a decent chap if you understand him—I find him faithful, discreet."

"Discreet!" echoed Helen mockingly. "I beg to differ."

"What do you mean?"

"I mean that you are blinded in the man. Discreet indeed! Only the other day I caught him at your desk reading a letter which you had left there."

"A letter?" exclaimed Kenneth, looking up in surprise. "What letter?"

"The letter from your agent at Cape Town, telling of the astonishing diamond find, and suggesting that an officer of the Company be sent out to bring home the big stone—the letter you read at the director's meeting and which decided them to send you out there."

Kenneth bit his lip. Quickly he said:

"I'm sorry he saw that. It was careless of me to leave it around. Are you sure he was reading it?"

"He had a pencil and paper in hand and appeared to be copying from the letter. When he saw me, he crushed the paper up in his hand and turned away."

Kenneth gave an expressive whistle.

"The deuce you say! The fellow's smarter than I took him to be. All the more reason why I should take him along with me. Then I'm sure he can't tell tales out of school. I—. Hush, here he is!"

The door opened cautiously and there entered a man about thirty years of age, of medium height and slightly, even delicately, built. That he was a Frenchman was apparent even at a glance. The dark closely cropped hair, worn in the so-called pompadour or military style, the pale, saturnine features, the manner and general bearing all loudly proclaimed his Gallic nationality. His smooth shaven face showed a firm mouth with bloodless lips so thin as to be hardly perceptible. His eyes, when they could be seen at all, were greenish in color, and small and restless as those of a ferret. He advanced into the room with the obsequious deferential manner which in all well-trained servants becomes second nature, moving across the thickly carpeted floor with the rapidity and noise-lessness of a snake.

"Where have you been, Francois?" demanded Kenneth sharply.

The valet stopped short, as if struck by a blow, but he did not stand still. His nervous thin hands and lean body were in constant motion, although he did not stir from the one spot. In every involuntary movement and gesture there was something that suggested the feline. When spoken to or given an order he replied respectfully and obeyed with alacrity, but when addressed he listened always with eyes averted. This had always exasperated Helen. She could not recall him ever looking her straight in the face. For that reason alone, if, for no other, she disliked and distrusted him, thinking not unnaturally that a man, who is afraid to let his eyes meet another's, must be plotting in his mind some treachery which he fears his direct gaze may betray. His furtive glances went quickly from master to mistress. Something in their attitude, the suddenness with which they interrupted their conversation told him that they had been talking about him.

"Did you hear me?" demanded Kenneth again. "Where have you been? You knew there was this packing to be done."

The man's eyes flashed resentfully, but he replied civilly:

"Oui, monsieur, but monsieur forgets. Monsieur told me I must go to ze tailor."

Kenneth's frown disappeared. Yes, it was true. He had sent him to the tailor. Quick to make amends for an injustice, he said more amiably:

"That's right. I had forgotten. What did they say?"

"Ze suits will be delivered in half hour."

"Very well. When they come, you will know which trunk to put them in."

"Oui, monsieur."

"And then, when my trunks are ready you had better hustle with your own packing. There's no time to be lost. The steamer sails at 11 o'clock to-morrow morning."

"Oui, monsieur."

Quietly, stealthily, the valet retraced his cat-like steps and opening the door retired as noiselessly as he had come.

CHAPTER III

When the valet had disappeared, Kenneth turned to his wife with a chuckle.

"Who was right? You made me scold him for nothing."

Helen shook her head.

"I detest the man. There is something crawly and repulsive about him. I can read evil in his face. Don't trust him, Kenneth. Remember, if anything goes wrong, don't blame me. I warned you. My instinct seldom fails."

Her husband laughed and, advancing, put his arm tenderly around his wife.

"I guess I'm able to take care of myself, dear. Don't let's discuss Francois any longer. Tell me about yourself. How are you going to amuse yourself while I'm away?"

Her head drooped on his breast and once more her eyes filled with tears. With affected carelessness which cost her a great effort, she replied:

"Oh, the time won't hang so heavy on my hands. It never does when one has resources within oneself. I'll read and ride and sew. I suppose I'll have plenty to do."

"Mr. Parker said he would drop in and look after you."

"Yes—tell him to come and see me very often. He's rather tiresome with his prosy talk, but he's a dear old soul."

With a mischievous twinkle in his eye her husband went on:

"It's not unlikely that Keralio will call, also."

"I hope not," she said quickly. "I'll soon show him he's not wanted."

Kenneth laughed. It amused him to see how set she was against the Italian. He did not know the man any too well. He had met him in a business way and the fellow had been of service, but he had not the slightest idea of making a friend of him. He rather suspected he was an adventurer although, a stranger in New York, no one knew anything against him. Protestingly he said:

"It's hardly fair to attack a man because he admires you."

"He shows his admiration in a most offensive way. If you could see the way he looks at me sometimes you'd be the first to resent it."

Kenneth laughed.

"Oh, you mustn't mind that. It's a way all foreigners have. They ogle women more from force of habit than any desire to effect a conquest. Besides, you won't be alone."

"No, I shall have Ray. She is excellent company—far jollier than I—"

Kenneth protested.

"No, she isn't by a long shot. Ray is all right as sisters-in-law go, but I'd never change you for her. I'm d—d if I would!"

Quickly Helen put her white hand over his mouth. With

mock severity she exclaimed:

"Kenneth! How can you be so profane? I hate to hear such language from you. Ray is the sweetest thing on earth. It's a shame she never got married. Oh, don't be uneasy on that score. We'll have a good time. We'll go to the theater. We'll have teas and little dinner parties. I'll invite some interesting men to meet her. I'd love to see her married to some nice man. There's Mr. Steell, for instance. He's rich, young, has a brilliant future—"

Kenneth made a grimace. Quickly he retorted:

"It's you he admires, not Ray. He will accept your invitation—less with the idea of letting Ray hook him in the matrimonial net, than for the opportunity it affords for a renewed flirtation with you. Oh, quite innocent, of course, but still a flirtation. Have I forgotten what close friends you used to be before I appeared on the scene?"

"And carried me off, a new Lochinvar come out of the West!" she laughed. "Oh, Kenneth, how can you be so foolish? It is absolutely indecent of you. I like Mr. Steell, and I think he likes me, but our friendship is purely platonic. I never give him a thought, I assure you."

"I know you don't, but I'm not so sure about him. He's a man and men are only human—"

"He's a gentleman," corrected Helen. "He never forgets that."

Kenneth gave a grunt of incredulity. Sulkily he said:

"All right—all right. Have a good time. Marry him to Ray. Perhaps it's safer that way. When he's my brother-in-law, he'll stop making sheep's eyes at my wife."

Helen laughed outright.

"You silly goose. I never suspected you of having a jealous streak in your nature. How could I prefer anyone to my handsome Kenneth?"

As she stood before him, playfully patting his cheek, her glance alighted on the solitary lock of gray hair in the center of his forehead. Toying with it, she went on:

"Isn't it strange that your hair should be white just in that place. I rather like it. It gives an added note of distinction to your face. I wonder what caused it."

Kenneth laughed.

"That's my trade mark. If ever I'm brought home on a stretcher you'll know me by that white lock."

Helen raised her hand in protest.

"Don't talk that way. Never jest about accidents. Sometimes they happen."

"Well—I said nothing. I only said that if you were ever in doubt about my identity, you would know me by my white lock."

She smiled, as she patted his cheek lovingly, and said:

"That would not be necessary, Ken dear. No matter how changed you looked, what disguise you wore, I should still know you."

"And if it wasn't me," he laughed, "but only someone who looked like me?"

"I could never be mistaken. The ring in the voice, the expression in the eyes—no woman who really loves could ever be deceived."

She had drawn nearer to him, her mouth upturned and tempting, her face with that gentle, wistful expression he was never able to resist. Throwing his arms impulsively about her, he clasped her passionately to his breast.

"Sweetheart," he whispered, "you don't know how dear you are to me!"

"Nor can you," she replied, as he smothered her with kisses, "ever realize what you are to me!"

Suddenly they were interrupted by a sound at the door behind them. Some one coughed discreetly. Quickly separating, Helen turned round. In some confusion she exclaimed:

"Hello, Ray. I thought you were out. When did you come in?"

"I was out. I have been shopping. I met Mr. Steell in the park and we had a lovely walk." Slyly she added: "I am afraid I returned too soon. I see you're both busy."

"Never too busy for you, Ray," smiled Helen trying to hide her confusion, while Kenneth grinned broadly.

The young girl laughed as she flung down on the sofa her muff and fur neck-piece. Roguishly she said:

"Lovemaking so early in the day. Aren't you ashamed of yourselves?"

Kenneth liked to tease his sister-in-law, but the young girl was quite his equal when it came to a battle of wits and it was not often that she gave him the opportunity.

"What time do you do your love making?" he demanded.

Her cheeks reddened a little as she retorted:

"I'm never so foolish. I leave that to you married people. My purpose in life is far more serious."

"Oh, come now," protested her brother-in-law, "I've noticed you and Steell spooning often enough."

Stylishly and tastefully dressed, her face beaming with animation, her eyes sparkling with intelligence, Kenneth's sister-in-law was a pretty, wholesome looking girl. She had beautiful blond hair like her sister, and fine, white teeth that told of good health and perfect digestion. Helen's junior only by three years, she was still unmarried and for the present at least seemed more inclined to remain single and partake of life's pleasures than incur the risks and responsibilities of matrimony. Not that she had been without offers. A girl as attractive and clever could hardly have failed to please the sterner sex. All sorts and conditions of men had prostrated themselves at her tiny, well-shod feet, but, capricious and headstrong, she would have none of them. She was what might be called a singular girl. She liked men, not because of their sex, but because their point of view was different, their grasp of things stronger than her own. One day she must marry. She knew that. It was, she insisted laughingly, an ignoble state of slavery, a humiliating, degrading condition of subjection to the male which every woman must endure, necessary perhaps, but an ordeal to be put off, something unpleasant to be postponed as long as possible, like the taking of a dose of unsavory physic or having a tooth pulled at the dentist's. Meantime, heart whole and fancy free, she enjoyed life to the limit and kept her admirers guessing.

"Oh, I saw such lovely things in the stores," exclaimed the young girl. "I wish I had the money to buy them all."

"You will have when I get back from South Africa," he laughed.

"Don't forget," she laughed. "I'll hold you to that promise. Helen is witness."

Arthur Hornblow

"I swear it!" he said with mock solemnity. "You shall have carte blanche in any Fifth Avenue shop to the amount of—$1.75."

"Will you be ready in time?" she laughed, looking around with dismay at the litter of open trunks.

"I won't, if you stay here chattering like a magpie."

"What time does the steamer sail?"

"Eleven o'clock," said Helen.

"We're all coming to see you off. Mr. Steell told me that he's coming, too."

"Not exactly to see me, I'm afraid," smiled Kenneth.

"Who else?" she retorted. "If you mean me, you're mistaken. He doesn't need to make the uncomfortable trip to Hoboken to see me."

Her brother-in-law smiled, amused at her petulance.

"My dear," he said, "you don't know what hardships a man will endure for the girl he's sweet on." With mock seriousness he went on: "Say sis, Helen and I have been having an argument. Who does Steell come here for—for you or for me?"

Ray burst into merry laughter.

"How silly you are, Ken. For me, of course. At least, I flatter myself that—" With a wink at her sister she added facetiously: "Of course, one never knows when dealing with these handsome men. And Helen is quite adorable. If I were a man, I should be crazy about her."

Helen held up a protesting finger.

"Don't talk like that, dear, or he'll believe you."

Kenneth laughed.

"Yes, I'm as jealous as Othello and quite as dangerous. Don't I look it?"

As he spoke, the front door-bell rang downstairs. Ray hastily took up her things.

"Here's company!"

"I hope not!" exclaimed Helen. "I'm in no mood to see anybody."

"I'll see them," whispered Ray, "and say you're out. It won't be the first fib I've told."

She ran lightly out of the room and upstairs, while Helen and her husband went on with the work of packing. They were just stooping together over a trunk when there came a rap on the door, and Francois appeared.

"A lady to see monsieur."

Kenneth looked puzzled.

"A lady? What lady?"

Helen laughed merrily. Triumphantly, she exclaimed:

"It's my turn now to be jealous."

"Not exactly a lady, monsieur. An elderly person."

"What's her name?"

"Mrs. Mary O'Connor."

Kenneth smiled broadly.

"Mary O'Connor, my old nurse. Well, well, show her right in." Turning to his wife he added quickly: "Dear old soul—no doubt she's heard I'm off to Africa and wishes to say good-bye."

An instant later an old woman bent with age and with a kindly face framed with silvery white hair came in, hands outstretched. Without any air of condescension on his part, Kenneth went forward to greet her. Through all the long stretch of years, from his boy days to his manhood he had never forgotten how kind Mary had been to him when a child, taking the place of the mother he had lost in infancy. A Christmas was never allowed to pass without a fat turkey for the old nurse and many a little present of money had accompanied the bird. The old woman's lips quivered as she said tremulously:

"It's a long way you're going, Mr. Kenneth."

"Oh, I'll soon be back, Mary," he rejoined jovially.

She shook her head.

"It's a long way and I'm getting old."

The promoter laughed boisterously. Leading her gently to a chair he exclaimed:

"Old! Nonsense; You're just as young to me now as when I first remember you."

The old lady smiled. Nodding her head feebly, she replied:

"When you used to play hide-and-seek with me. When I wanted to put you to bed you were nowhere to be found."

Helen laughed while Kenneth protested:

"Oh, come now, Mary, I wasn't so bad as that."

"No. You weren't bad—just lively and natural as all healthy children. You were always a better boy than your brother."

Helen looked up quickly.

"Your brother, Kenneth? I never heard you speak of a brother."

He looked at the old lady in amazement.

"My brother? What brother?"

The old lady smiled.

"That's so—you never knew. You were too young to remember. Yes, you had a brother—a twin brother. People hardly knew you apart. There was only one way in which your mother and I could tell."

"What was that?" demanded the promoter eagerly.

"He had a scar. He caught his hand in some machinery when a baby and it left a scar in the index finger of the left hand."

Transfixed, Kenneth listened open-mouthed. At last breaking the spell, he exclaimed:

"I never heard of him. You never spoke of him before."

"How should you remember?" went on the old woman. "It's many years ago. Your father and mother are dead. You have no relatives living. No one knows. But I know."

"Did he die?" asked Kenneth, deeply interested.

The old lady nodded affirmatively.

"I shall never forgive myself. It was my fault. You were playing together in the garden. I didn't dream either of you could come to harm. I went into the house for a moment to get something. When I came back your brother was gone—no trace of him anywhere. We never saw him again. Your father, heart-broken, offered a fortune for news of him. The police hunted high and low all over the country. There was no trace. Some gypsies had passed recently through the town. I always suspected them. That is thirty years ago and more."

"So it's not even known if he's dead," interrupted Kenneth eagerly.

The beldame shook her head sorrowfully, as she answered sagely:

"Oh, he's dead all right. That's sure. There was money left to him by your grandfather. For years the lawyers advertised for news of him. But it was no good. If he'd been alive, he'd have claimed his own."

"He might still be alive, yet unaware of his identity," broke in Helen, who was a keenly interested listener. She had been so accustomed to regard her husband as the only son of parents, both of whom were dead, that the mere possibility of his having a brother awakened her curiosity.

Still under the spell of the old woman's unexpected revelation, Kenneth had relapsed into a thoughtful silence. The surprising news had affected him strangely. So—he had had a brother—a twin brother, and all these years he had been in ignorance of the fact. Yet who could be nearer or dearer than a twin brother? Together they had lain under the same mother's heart. Together they had first seen the light and laughed in the sun. Ah, if he had only lived to be his comrade, his partner! With a brother at his side, to second him in his hazardous enterprises, he felt he would indeed be invincible. He could have conquered the world!

The old nurse held out a withered hand, and her eyes were moist with tears as she said:

"Good-bye, Mr. Kenneth. A safe journey to you. Keep out of danger. I'll be praying for the Lord to watch over you."

Helen turned away so they might not see her emotion. Kenneth laughed lightly as he kissed the old woman's cheek, and then, slipping a bank note into her hand, he said carelessly:

"All right, Mary, I'll be careful. I'll come back safe and sound,—never fear, and I'll bring you something nice,— perhaps a big diamond. Out in South Africa they pick 'em up like stones."

The old woman's eyes opened incredulously.

"Really, Mr. Kenneth?"

"Yes, really. Diamonds as big as apples. They're found every day. When I come back I'll have all sorts of adventures to tell you about. Who knows? I might even run across this twin-brother of mine. Stranger things have happened."

"Diamonds as big as apples," she echoed. "Do you mean that, Mr. Kenneth?"

He laughed.

"Indeed I do! Some of the gems are as big as cocoanuts. Didn't you hear of that wonderful diamond we found the other day? It's worth a million dollars."

The old woman opened her eyes and gaped with astonishment.

"A million dollars, Mr. Kenneth!"

"Yes, a million dollars. What's more, I'll soon be able to show it to you, Mary. My trip out to South Africa is ostensibly for the purpose of negotiating for more land. The real purpose of my journey is to bring home this astonishing stone."

"But how will you carry it, Mr. Kenneth? A stone worth a million dollars must be big as a house."

Kenneth laughed.

"No—no, Mary. It can easily go in my waistcoat pocket. But for safety's sake it won't. I don't mind letting you into my confidence. I'm to have a secret bottom made in—"

Before he could complete the sentence, Helen quickly clapped her hand over his mouth, and he had not yet recovered from his astonishment when she sprang to the door and opened it. The movement was so sudden and unexpected that a man who had been leaning against it, fell all his length into the room. It was Francois, the French valet.

"*Excusez*," he stammered, "I stumbled."

Kenneth stared first at the servant, then at his wife. Slowly he began to comprehend. Turning to the Frenchman he demanded angrily:

"What were you doing behind that door?"

"*Excusez.* I came back to ask monsieur how many shirts I pack."

Thoroughly aroused, the promoter pointed to the door. Sternly he said:

"Get out of here—you fool! If you don't know your business, I'll get some one else who does."

The Frenchman beat a rapid retreat. There was a malevolent look on his face, but he murmured respectfully enough:

"*Oui, monsieur.*"

Kenneth turned to his wife.

"What did he come back for?" he demanded.

"He was listening—behind the door," she replied calmly.

CHAPTER IV

The dirty, sullen waters of the harbor washed lazily against the black, precipitous sides of the giant liner which, under a full head of steam, vibrated with suppressed energy, straining at mighty cables as if impatient to start on her long and hazardous voyage across the tumbling seas. A raw, piercing northeaster, howling dismally above the monotonous creaking and puffing of the donkey-engine, swept through the cheerless, draughty dock, chilling the spectators to the marrow. The sun, vainly trying to break through the banks of leaden-colored clouds, cast a grayish pall over land and sky. A day it was of sinister portent, that could not fail to have a depressing effect on sailor and landlubber alike.

Yet unpropitious skies and chilly wind did not appear to keep people at home. The steamer was crowded, both with those who were sailing and those who were not. The gangways, staterooms were overrun not only by passengers, but by all sorts of visitors curious to get a glimpse of the luxurious liner. The first-class saloon, heaped high on all sides with American Beauty roses and orchids, looked as gay and full of color as a florist's shop.

"Isn't it perfectly stunning? How I adore ships!" exclaimed Ray, eager to see everything.

Keeping close together, the two young women with difficulty elbowed their way through the excited throng. They were anxious to rejoin Kenneth whom they had left in the stateroom giving instructions to Francois, and they began to be afraid they might lose him in the crush. Delighted at everything she saw, Ray could not contain herself.

"Oh, how I wish I were going! Why doesn't Ken take me?"

Helen turned to her in mock despair.

"If you went, what would I do? Who would take care of me?"

"I would," said a masculine voice close by.

The women turned quickly.

A tall, fair man still in his thirties, had stopped and raised his hat.

"Why, it's Mr. Steell!" exclaimed Ray, her pleasure at the meeting betraying itself in the tone of her voice.

"Do you doubt my ability to take care of you? Could any man wish for a more congenial task?"

"Flatterer!" laughed Helen. Cordially she added: "I'm awfully glad to see you. It was very good of you to come and see Ken off."

"Nonsense," exclaimed the newcomer. "I wanted to come—if only to make sure he wouldn't change his mind. I'm as anxious to see those diamonds as you are."

"Hush!" said Helen putting up her finger to her mouth while Ray's attention was momentarily diverted elsewhere. "No one knows—not even Ray. It's a great secret."

An anxious look passed over the young man's face. He hadn't approved of this South African trip. It was wholly unnecessary. In his opinion his old chum was taking a great risk.

"That's right," he muttered. "You can't be too careful."

In metropolitan legal circles Wilbur Steell was looked upon as the coming man. His success in the courts had given him a wide reputation before he was five and thirty, and his gifts as a public speaker, his strong, aggressive personality made more than one political leader anxious to secure his services. Already he was mentioned as district attorney. Even the Governorship might have been his for the asking. But he showed no liking for politics. His sympathies leaned more towards the literary, intellectual life. Having all the money he needed, he preferred to keep out of the social and political maelstrom, leading a quiet life, following his own tastes and inclinations. Matchmaking mammas saw in him a prize, but so far he had shown no disposition to marry. He cultivated few people, in fact, was considered somewhat of a misanthrope. Kenneth he had known all his life. They were boys together, and the Traynors were among the few on whom he called frequently. He made no secret of his attraction for Ray, and the young girl liked him as well as she chose to like anybody. He had qualities, not usually met with in successful men, that made a strong appeal to her—fine ideals, and a purpose in life. She liked his seriousness, finding him different in this respect from any other man she knew. She felt he admired her, but he did not make love to her and she was grateful to him for that. She liked his society and never tired of discussing with him sociology and other subjects in which both were interested.

"When does the steamer sail?" interrupted Ray anxiously, as if afraid that they might go off with her on board.

"In half an hour," said the lawyer. "They ring a warning bell. There is plenty of time. Where's Kenneth?"

"Down below in his stateroom—wrestling with baggage," replied Helen. "He said he would join us here."

"Well, suppose we sit down a bit," he suggested.

"Yes—that will be jolly," exclaimed Ray.

The lawyer pulled up three steamer chairs and sitting down, they watched the crowd which had already begun to thin out. The novelty of the scene held both women fascinated. The constant bustle and excitement, the going and coming of well-groomed men and women, the little scraps of conversation overheard, interested them both beyond measure. Helen studied each individual couple, wondering who they were, how long married, if they were happy, where they were going to. She wondered if that coarse, loudly dressed woman really cared for her husband, or if this brutal looking man with insolent stare of the libertine, illtreated his delicate little wife. She herself could not understand marriage without genuine affection on both sides. Any such intimate relation as the marriage tie involved must surely be repellent and abhorrent to any self-respecting woman unless love were there to sanction and sanctify it.

Ray glanced at her sister and laughed.

"Why so serious, Helen? He hasn't gone yet."

Helen sighed.

"But he soon will be. I wish he were here instead of downstairs."

Ray protested.

"Please be nautically correct. Remember we are on a ship. You don't say 'downstairs'; you say 'below.'"

Mr. Steell turned round with a smile.

"I had no idea you were so well posted in sailor's parlance."

The young girl laughed.

"Oh, you don't know half my accomplishments. I'm cleverer than you give me credit for."

The young man leaned half over the chair as he whispered:

"I wouldn't dare tell you how clever I think you."

"Why?"

"Because—of my own peace of mind."

Helen broke in on the conversation. Addressing the lawyer, she said:

"Now Kenneth is away, we shall expect you to come to the house very often."

The lawyer bowed.

"It's always a pleasure to call."

"Be sure to come next Sunday evening. I expect some friends. We'll have some music."

"May I bring someone?"

"Certainly. Any friend of yours is welcome."

"Who is it?" asked Ray impertinently. "Male or female?"

"I believe it's a male," smiled the lawyer. "It looks like a male and talks like one." More seriously he went on: "His name is Dick Reynolds. He has just passed his bar examination and is practicing temporarily in my office. His people live out West and being alone here, he is glad enough to have somewhere to go."

"Bring him by all means," exclaimed Ray. "Has he any accomplishments—apart from being a male?"

"Yes—he plays the piano indifferently, and tennis admirably. He swims like a fish, and can run like a hare. But his best accomplishment is a gift that one seldom sees developed—"

"What is that?" exclaimed both his listeners at once.

"He is a born detective—a regular Sherlock Holmes in real life. I have tested him several times with extraordinary results. I have given him the most difficult cases to unravel. He has found the solution in every one."

Ray clapped her hands.

"Oh, I love that," she said. "Don't forget to invite him. Only the trouble is we have nothing to unravel."

"I have a skein of silk," interrupted Helen facetiously.

Suddenly the lawyer stopped speaking and quickly sitting up in his chair stared intently in the distance at a face in the crowd which had caught his eye.

"Who is it?" demanded Ray, her woman's jealousy aroused.

"I may be mistaken," he replied, "but I thought I saw your friend Signor Keralio."

Helen looked up quickly.

"My friend?" she exclaimed. "He's no friend of mine. I wonder what he's doing here. He can't be sailing."

"He's up to no good, I wager that," growled the lawyer.

"You don't like him either, do you?" smiled Ray.

"Does anyone?" he answered. "I don't see how Kenneth can have anything to do with such a cheap type of adventurer."

Helen hastened to explain.

"Ken doesn't care for him at all, only they are both interested in the same business deal—a silver mine in Mexico. Ken bought stock and Keralio is the only man he knows connected with it. That's why."

The lawyer gave vent to a grunt of disgust.

"If Keralio has anything to do with it, good-bye to Ken's money. In my opinion the fellow's a crook."

Suddenly Helen pointed to a spot away down at the other end of the deck.

"Yes—you're right—there he is—behind that third lifeboat. He's talking to some one."

The lawyer looked in the direction indicated.

"Yes—and do you see the secretive way in which they're talking—hiding behind that boat, as if so that no one might see them. They're plotting some mischief, you may be sure of that. Who's the other fellow?"

Helen strained her eyes to see.

"I can't see his face. Oh, yes I can—why—it's our Francois—Kenneth's valet. What can they be talking about? I don't trust that valet. Only the other day I caught him reading some letters. I warned Ken about him; but he insists he is faithful—I wonder what they can have in common? He used to be in Signor Keralio's employ."

The lawyer shook his head ominously. Gravely he said:

"That fellow Keralio will bear watching. I think I'll put my Sherlock Holmes on his track."

Ray laughed.

"Oh, that would be exciting—a drama in real life. Please do—"

"Good morning, ladies!" said a voice close at hand. "Good morning, Mr. Steell."

All looked up. A tall, elderly man with white hair, distinguished looking and fashionably dressed, had stopped.

"Why, it's Mr. Parker!" exclaimed Helen holding out her hand. "You came to see Kenneth off?"

"Yes—where is he?"

"In his stateroom—attending to his baggage. He'll be here directly."

"I must see him at once."

"Anything important?"

"Very important, indeed," replied the newcomer.

Helen jumped up, all flushed from excitement.

"Please tell me what it is?" she exclaimed.

The old gentleman drew a telegram from his pocket.

"I've just received this from our agent in Cape Town. Another diamond of extraordinary size has been picked up. It weighs over 2,000 carats and is calculated to be worth five hundred thousand dollars. That's the second stone of extraordinary size that we have found. Possibly there is some exaggeration in the reports, but there is no doubt whatever that we are on the verge of discoveries little short of sensational. Meantime, the treasury of the Americo-African Mining Company has been enriched by at least a million. When Kenneth returns to New York with these wonderful gems in his possession, there is likely to be a boom in the company's shares."

The old gentleman spoke glibly, even eloquently and it was obvious that he was sincere and not talking for effect. It was, indeed, largely due to his distinguished air, and fine oratorical powers that Cornelius Winthrop Parker had been elected president of the Americo-African Mining Company, with fine offices in New York and London and stockholders in every country under the sun. Trained for the ministry and enjoying a wide acquaintance but a slim income, he had found the business of stock company promotion more profitable than preaching the gospel, and when Traynor had first gone to him with the suggestion that a company be formed to take up the large tract of Transvaal land where precious stones had actually been found he was not slow to grasp at the unusual opportunity. He managed cleverly the preliminary publicity campaign. The company was promptly organized and success-fully floated, the public snapping as eagerly at the shares as a fish at the bait. It was only logical to infer, therefore, that when Kenneth returned to New York with actual proof of the company's suddenly acquired wealth in his possession, the stock would soar above par. With this pleasing prospect in view, it was not surprising that Mr. Parker wore to-day his most engaging smile.

Ray looked up in surprise.

"What!" she exclaimed. "Kenneth to bring home the diamonds? This is the first I heard of it. Helen never told me."

"Hush!" said Mr. Parker, holding up his handy warningly. "Some one might hear you." Continuing, he said blandly:

"Of course not, my dear lady, of course not. Your sister is far too discreet and clever a woman to disclose her husband's plans to the world. There are some things a man must keep secret from everyone—even from his wife. It would have been the height of folly to make any such announcement from the housetops. The highways are full of rogues; even the walls have ears. Some crook might have learned of our plans and acted accordingly. Kenneth might be followed to South Africa, shadowed till he has the gems in his possession and then waylaid and murdered. Remember, he will have stones in his waistcoat pocket worth a million. Do you suppose desperate men will stop at anything to secure such a prize?"

Ray turned to her sister.

"Did you know?"

Helen nodded.

"Yes, and it has made me very unhappy. It is terrible that he is taking such risks." Turning to Mr. Parker she asked apprehensively: "Do you think he will run any danger?"

The old gentleman shook his head.

"Of course not, my dear lady. It is preposterous to even think of such a thing. We have kept the matter too secret. Don't be uneasy. He will come to no harm." Raising his hat, he added: "Excuse me, ladies. I'll go and find Kenneth and bring him to you."

The next instant he was swallowed up by the crowd.

Helen, uneasy at her husband's prolonged absence, suggested that they go below and join him.

Suddenly a stentorian voice called out:

"All ashore—all ashore!"

Quickly, Helen jumped to her feet, only to bump into Kenneth, who at that moment ran up, followed by Mr. Parker.

"All ashore, dear," he said hastily, "you had better go."

She made no reply, but averted her head so he might not see her red eyes.

All about them the bustle and excitement was bewildering. People pushed this way and that in their efforts to reach the gangway.

The siren sounded its last deep toned blasts of warning; the final greetings were exchanged.

Tall and handsome looking in his tourist knicker-bockers and close fitting steamer cap, Kenneth held both Helen's hands in his. Ray and Mr. Parker, under the pretence of visiting the anchor weighed, had discreetly withdrawn. Francois, the valet, could be seen in the distance, making signals to some one on shore. Husband and wife were standing alone behind one of the big ventilators, Helen glad that no one saw them, ashamed that anyone should detect the big tears she was unable to control. How she had dreaded this moment of actual parting, this ordeal of saying good-bye!

"You'll write every day, won't you?" she asked in choking voice.

Tenderly he drew her to him.

"Every day, sweetheart."

"And you'll come back safe to me?"

"I'll come back safe to you."

Bravely she forced back the tears that blinded her. Gently she murmured:

"I'll wait for you, Kenneth. I shall count the days, every moment, until you return. I never realized till now how much we are to each other. I'll pray for you, Kenneth; I'll pray God that He watch over and protect you."

He said nothing, but drew her toward him. Looking searchingly into her eyes, he said half in jest, half in earnest:

"You'll be true, always true!"

Gravely she answered:

"Always—until death!"

"You'll look at no other man."

"How can you be so foolish, Ken dear? I see no one but you. I hear no voice but yours. You are my life, my soul. When you return you'll find me here, at this same dock, arms outstretched, waiting, just waiting."

The bell rang.

"All ashore! All ashore!"

He bent low. His mouth met hers in one deep, lingering kiss.

"God bless you, darling."

"Good-bye, Ken, good-bye."

The next thing she knew she was back on the dock among a crowd of spectators waving hats and handkerchiefs—the women weeping, the men shouting and gesticulating.

The passengers stood at the rail, waving frantic adieux in return. The siren sounded deep-toned blasts of warning to the smaller river craft to get out of the way. The huge vessel strained and trembled, vibrating more violently as she gradually began to glide into the open. Assisted by a fleet of energetic tugs she finally swung clear and pointed her nose eastward. Slowly, majestically, the leviathan moved out to sea.

It was bad enough to see him go at all, but to have him sail on such a gloomy day as this, with not a ray of sunshine to cheer him on the way, was more than Helen could bear. Blinded by tears she stood kissing her hand to the familiar figure now only faintly discernible on the fast receding steamship, and she stood there long after every one else had left the dock watching until the *Mauretania* was only a speck in the horizon.

CHAPTER V

Sunday evenings at Mrs. Traynor's were always enjoyable. No formal invitations were issued. Friends just dropped in as they felt inclined. There was good music, excellent tea *a la Russe* and always a number of interesting people.

To-night, the second Sunday since Kenneth went away, promised to be duller than usual. Mr. Steell was there, of course, and he had brought Dick Reynolds, a slightly built, shrewd looking young man with glasses, who kept everybody amused with exciting stories of the underworld. Yet, for all the animation, there was an atmosphere of gloom in the air, an indefinable sense of depression which all felt and could not explain. The lawyer, Dick, and Ray were in a corner carrying on an animated discussion. Helen, her mind preoccupied, her thoughts hundreds of miles away with the loved absent one, sat quietly at the piano, running her fingers lightly over the keys, her thoughts many leagues distant with the man who had carried her heart away with him.

Her face was pale, her expression grave. Why had Kenneth's going away affected her like this? She had not had a moment's peace of mind since his departure. She could not sleep. Horrible dreams and thoughts haunted her all night. Some danger threatened, that she felt instinctively. Something dreadful was going to happen. What it was, she did not know. But it was something that threatened her happiness, perhaps her life or Kenneth's—. At the mere thought a shiver ran through her, and a convulsive sob rose in her throat, almost choking her. Not until this moment had she fully realized how much she loved him.

A sudden burst of laughter at the other end of the room aroused her from her reverie. Looking up, she asked:

"What are you all so amused about?"

Ray smiled as she replied:

"We're arguing about dual personalities. Mr. Steell insists that there is no such thing. Mr. Reynolds agrees with him. He is wrong of course. I know of several well-authenticated cases, and the medical records are there to back me up."

"Exactly what do you mean by dual personality?" demanded the lawyer.

Ray returned to the attack, while Helen, amused, rose from the piano and went over to listen to the argument.

"I mean that a person we know well may suddenly cease being that person and assume a personality entirely different."

Mr. Steell laughed derisively.

"Does the patient change her or his skin?"

"No, the change is wholly mental. Although in fact, the new mental attitude does result in certain physical modifications. For instance, a person who in his normal condition may be most punctilious and neat in his dress is likely to become unkempt and slovenly in the new character he unconsciously assumes."

"Have you ever encountered any such dual personalities?"

"Personally, no. But I have heard of them, and physicians often encounter them in their practice."

The lawyer shrugged his shoulders as he turned to Helen.

"What do you think about it?" he asked, with an incredulous smile.

"About what?"

"These so-called dual personalities."

Before his hostess could answer, the drawing-room door opened and Mr. Parker entered. Helen rose and went forward to greet the president of the Americo-African Mining Company.

"Oh, Mr. Parker, how are you? I am so glad you came to see us."

The visitor advanced smiling into the room. With a salute to all present, he asked cheerily:

"Well, what news of the wanderer?"

Helen sighed.

"None as yet."

The visitor chuckled as he crossed the room to shake hands with Ray and Mr. Steell.

"Oh, well you must be patient. He'll soon be there, and then we shall hear wonderful tales."

"What's the latest news from the seat of war—I mean the mines?" asked Ray roguishly.

Mr. Parker smiled.

"Everything is going well, thank you."

"No new big finds?" demanded Mr. Steell.

The president laughed. Shaking his head, he said:

"We can't expect to make such finds every day. If we often picked up stones of that size, we'd soon own all the wealth in the world."

"More likely," retorted Ray quickly, "that diamonds would become so cheap that children would buy them for marbles."

Mr. Steell looked interested.

"What is the real market value of the two big gems you have already picked up?"

The president looked at him for a moment in silence. Then, slowly, he said:

"A very conservative estimate is $1,200,000 for both stones. They are the purest white. There are larger stones in the world, but none of finer quality."

"What do you expect to do with them?"

"First, they will be brought here and exhibited in their crude state. You can easily realize the value to our company of such a gigantic advertisement. Crowds will flock to see the wonderful crystals. The newspapers all over the country will give them the widest publicity. After everybody has seen them, we shall probably send them to Amsterdam to be cut."

"Then, what will you do with them?"

"To tell you the truth, we have not made up our minds. Such very large stones have really no commercial value. Take for instance the famous Cullinan, the wonder of the modern world. That gem was so huge that it was of no real value to the owners; so, unable to realize on it themselves, they induced the

Transvaal government to buy it and present it to the King of England. We shall try to be a little more practical. Our first duty is to our stockholders. We shall probably have the stones cut up into a number of smaller stones, on which we shall be able to realize a large sum. It's a rare stroke of good fortune for us."

Helen had said nothing, but stood listening in silence. It was less of the money involved in the adventure that she was thinking than of her husband's safety.

"Suppose Kenneth loses the gems?" she faltered.

The old gentleman laughed.

"There's no fear of him losing them. He may have to fight for them, but he'll never lose them I know him too well for that."

Helen's eyes opened wide.

"He may have to fight for them," she echoed. "Do you mean that?"

"No—no, of course not," said the president hastily. "No one will even know he has them in his possession. We have kept the matter very quiet."

Mr. Steell shrugged his shoulders. Drily he said:

"Oh, I guess Ken is big enough to take care of himself. It does look as if it were tempting Providence to carry loose on one's person valuables for so large an amount, but it's hardly likely that any of the denizens of the underworld know of his departure. Still less that he is carrying a million loose in his clothes. I don't see that there's any reason to worry."

"That's precisely my opinion," said a musical voice immediately behind them.

All started and looked up. Everyone had been so intent on the conversation that they had not noticed a man who had entered the room.

He was a tall, dark-complexioned man of five and thirty with strong, stern features, which, in repose, were actually forbidding. The mouth, partly concealed by a long, bristling moustache, was firm, suggesting relentless will power, and his eyes, restless, keen and searching, had taken in every person there long before anyone was aware of his presence. He was fashionably, even elegantly dressed, and on his left hand he wore a solitaire of uncommon size and luster. His hair, carefully curled, scented and parted, was extraordinarily dark, contrasting sharply with the unusual pallor of his face. He spoke low and musically, with a slight foreign accent.

Helen started involuntarily on hearing the sound of his voice, and a cloud passed momentarily over her face. It lasted only a moment. She was too tactful, too much the woman of the world not to greet with at least apparent cordiality any visitor under her roof, no matter how unwelcome he might really be. Turning quickly, she advanced and held out her hand.

"How do you do, Signor Keralio? How you startled us! I did not hear you come in."

The newcomer's black eyes flashed, and his thin lips parted in a smile as he bent low and ceremoniously kissed his hostess' hand in continental fashion. Fond, as are most men of the Latin race, of making extravagant compliments, he murmured softly:

"Your tiny ears, Madam, were not intended to distinguish such gross sounds as ordinary mortal's footsteps. Dainty and delicately fashioned as the shells strewn along the beach, they were modeled only to listen to the gods or re-echo the music of the murmuring sea." Apologetically he added:

"But I'm afraid I intrude. Possibly you discuss family affairs—"

A look of annoyance crossed Helen's face. Quickly withdrawing her hand, she said:

"Oh, not at all. We were only talking about my husband. You know he sailed for South Africa two weeks ago. This is Mr. Steell, Signor Keralio. I think you know my sister. Mr. Parker—Signor Keralio."

The old gentleman nodded affably, and, putting on his glass, scrutinized the newcomer narrowly. The president of the Americo-African Mining Company had always made it a point not to neglect any chance introduction. He had no idea who the visitor was, but he looked prosperous. Possibly with a little careful manipulation, he might be induced to invest in some A. A. M. stock. Holding out his hand, he said affably:

"Signor Keralio—Let me see. Where have I heard that name before?"

Ray came to the rescue.

"Signor Keralio is the well-known fencing master."

A look of disappointment came over the president's face. Only a fencing master? Ugh! He was hardly worth bothering about. He wondered whether the business were profitable and if all fencing masters dressed like millionaires and had such polished manners. Helen explained:

"Signor Keralio is a friend of my husband. Kenneth enjoys fencing, and Signor Keralio is his teacher."

"Oh, yes, to be sure," smiled Mr. Parker. "Capital idea— splendid exercise. I'd try it myself, only I'm afraid I'd do my adversary some injury."

The Italian gave a low chuckle. With veiled irony, he said:

Arthur Hornblow

"Monsieur is right. He no doubt has a good eye, a supple wrist. An encounter might be very unpleasant for his opponent."

Ray, unable to control her mirth, hastily beat a retreat, followed more leisurely by Mr. Steell, and taking refuge at the far end of the room sat down at the piano, and began to play softly a Chopin nocturne.

Waving the newcomer to a seat, Mr. Parker offered him a cigar, which the fencing master, with a courteous bow, asked his hostess' permission to smoke.

"By all means," she said, "and with your permission I'll leave you gentlemen alone a few moments. I have a letter to finish. It must go tonight to catch the boat."

"It's to your husband, I wager," said Keralio, with a sardonic smile.

"An easy guess," she retorted. "I write him every day."

The fencing master gave a sigh as he exclaimed:

"Ah, such devotion is truly beautiful! Why have I never known such love as that?"

"Perhaps you never deserved it!" she retorted.

Mr. Parker chuckled.

"That's what we in the American vernacular call 'a knock-out.'"

Helen laughed lightly. There was a swish of silken petticoats, and she disappeared in an alcove, where she sat down at a desk. Keralio looked after her with undisguised admiration and puffed his cigar in silence for a few moments. Then he said:

"It's a big job which you and Traynor are doing out there in South Africa. I see by the papers that you've already made some valuable finds."

He appeared unconcerned, and looked narrowly at his *vis a vis* to see what effect his words had on him, possibly to draw him out. But Mr. Parker was too old a bird to be caught napping, even by a clever adventurer. Instantly on his guard, he said carelessly:

"The outlook is very bright, very promising indeed. Our stockholders are quite satisfied, and it is likely that we shall make good money. But of course everything is in the experimental stage as yet."

"But you have found diamonds—big diamonds?"

"Oh, yes," replied the president with affected carelessness; "we have picked up a few stones. As I told you, the prospects are very promising."

"But haven't you recently made some extraordinary finds?"

Mr. Parker shook his head.

"No—nothing worth mentioning.'"

Keralio smiled skeptically.

"Isn't your memory somewhat at fault, cher monsieur? Surely you haven't forgotten the two stones of enormous size just picked up—finds of sensational importance. The newspapers have been full of the story."

Mr. Parker made a deprecatory gesture.

"Pshaw! My dear sir, you ought to know what newspaper talk is worth! No yarn is too fantastic to print so long as it sells their papers. We found two stones of fair size, it is true, but to say that they are of priceless value is a gross exaggeration."

The Italian eyed his companion closely. Significantly he said:

"They're valuable enough, however, to justify you in refusing to trust their shipment to ordinary channels and in going to the expense of sending to South Africa one of your officers to whom is confided the task of bringing the gems home."

"How did you know that?" demanded Mr. Parker, surprised.

"There is very little I do not know," smiled Keralio ironically, as he blew a ring of cigar smoke up to the ceiling.

His curiosity aroused, the president of the A. A. M. Co. was about to question his companion farther, but at that moment Helen rose from the desk and came toward them.

"I'm not in the humor to write now," she said. "I'd rather talk." Sitting in a chair near them, she added quickly: "Won't you let me get you some tea?"

Both men shook their heads. Mr. Parker rose. With a mischievous twinkle in his eye, he said:

"I'll go over to the others and take a hand at bridge. I want to make some money, Signor—I'll leave you to entertain Mrs. Traynor."

With a courteous salutation to his hostess, a graceful act of chivalrous politeness of which he was a past master, Mr. Parker crossed the room in the direction of the card table.

CHAPTER VI

An awkward silence followed the president's departure. Helen would have detained him had she dared. Being alone with Keralio was very distasteful to her. Ill at ease in such close proximity to this man, whom she feared even more than she disliked, she sat still without saying a word. Presently between puffs of his cigar, he said:

"You really don't mind my smoking?"

"Oh, not at all."

He bowed and again relapsed into silence. She looked at him sideways and wondered why this foreigner had always inspired her with such dislike. His manner was courteous, and he was decidedly handsome. He had white teeth and fine eyes. They were bold eyes, but so were the eyes of other men. They had a habit of looking a woman through and through. She always felt embarrassed under his close scrutiny. It seemed to her as if he were undressing her mentally and took pleasure in surveying critically and admirably every part of her as a connoisseur examines a statue. She had an uncomfortable feeling when near him. She was afraid to look straight in his eyes, afraid that possibly he might be able to throw some spell over her, exert some hypnotic influence that she would not be able to resist. She considered him a seductive, dangerous man, the kind of man every pure woman, every wife who wishes to remain faithful to her marriage vows should avoid.

Suddenly while she was looking at him, he turned his head toward her. Before she could prevent it their eyes met.

He did not avert his gaze, but kept his eyes fixed on hers as if trying to awaken in her some of his own ardor. She tried to look away, but she could not. He seemed to hold her there by sheer force of will power. Frightened, she started to tremble in every limb. Yet, to her astonishment, she had no feeling of anger or resentment. It seemed quite natural that this man should gaze at her in this intimate, caressing way. She found herself taking pleasure in it. Her vanity was gratified. If he looked at her so persistently, it must be that he thought her pretty. Her face began to burn, her bosom heaved, a strange sensation that heretofore only her husband had been able to arouse, came over her. And still his eyes were on hers, caressing, voluptuous.

At the other end of this room the game of bridge was still in progress. Ray was winning, as usual, and amusing the men with her wit and vivaciousness. Mr. Steell had glanced over in their direction several times, and he saw enough to convince him that the attentions of the fencing master were unwelcome to their hostess. Had he caught Helen's eye, had she made the slightest sign that she was being annoyed, he would have instantly left the game and gone over to the window, if only to break up the tete-a-tete, but she did not once look up. Suddenly he remembered what had been suggested on the boat. It was an idea. Ray at that moment got up to get some tea, and, profiting by the opportunity, the lawyer leaned over and whispered:

"Say, Dick, you see that chap over there."

The young man looked up.

"Who—the signor?"

"Yes. What do you know about him?"

"Nothing good—although nothing very bad for that matter. He's a dark horse—keeps pretty much to himself. He's well known in the gay resorts, in the gambling houses and where they play the ponies."

"What's his reputation?"

"He's known as a liberal spender. He's always flashing big rolls of money—"

"Where does he get it—not from the fencing school?"

"No—that's only a blind."

The lawyer lowered his voice.

"Dick, my boy, that fellow will bear watching, and you're the man to do it."

"You want him shadowed?"

"Yes—find out where he goes, who he knows. My opinion is that he belongs to an international band of crooks—possibly counterfeiters, smugglers, or blackmailers. If you land him behind the bars you'll deserve well of your country."

Dick glanced once or twice in the direction of the object of their conversation, who, quite unconscious of their scrutiny, was still talking earnestly to Helen. The young man smiled, his chest expanded with satisfaction, and grimly he said:

"Leave him to me."

Quite unconscious of the attention he attracted, the Italian turned to Helen.

"You miss your husband very much?"

"Yes—terribly."

"It must be lonely for you."

"It is," she sighed.

"Yet you have your sister."

"Can a sister replace a husband?"

He gave a low, musical laugh.

"No—not a sister. A lover is preferable."

Quickly she retorted:

"My husband is my lover—-my lover is my husband."

He laughed, as he said:

"It sounds very pretty, but you must admit that it is rather banal."

"In what way?"

He flecked the ash from his cigar.

"You are too pretty, too charming a woman to be commonplace. Really it spoils you—"

Ignoring his compliments, she persisted.

"Do you mean I am commonplace because I call Kenneth my lover. What other lover should I or any other woman happily married have? I am faithful to him—he is loyal to me."

He gave a little mocking laugh, and was silent. How she hated him for that laugh! After a pause he said quietly and suggestively:

"I am sure you are faithful to him—"

For a moment she looked at him without speaking, eager to resent the implied imputation on her husband, yet unwilling to give the slanderer the satisfaction of seeing that his thrust had carried home. Concealing as best she could her growing irritation, she said calmly:

"Don't you suppose *he* also is faithful to me?"

Again that horrible, cynical smile. Fixing her with his piercing dark eyes, and, in a manner, the significance of which could not escape her, he said:

"Don't seek to know too much, Madam. To paraphrase a famous saying: 'It's a wise woman who knows her own husband.'"

Coloring with anger, she said:

"You mean—"

"Just what I say—that a woman, a wife cannot possibly be sure of her husband's fidelity. Think how different are the conditions. The wife, no matter if her temperament be warm or cold, is always at home, surrounded by prying eyes, rarely beset by temptation. The husband is often away, he goes on business journeys that free him temporarily from the chains which keep him in good behavior. If he is good looking, the women look at him, flirt with him. It is inevitable. The chances are that he succumbs to the first adventure—no matter how exemplary a husband he may be at home. If he is a man—of unusual character, he passes through the fire unscathed; if he is—just a man, he is attracted to the candle like the proverbial moth and sometimes singes his wings—"

She looked at him keenly for a moment as if trying to read on his sphinx-like face if he knew more about Kenneth than he admitted, and then with forced calmness she said:

"In your opinion, Signor Keralio—is my husband a man—of

unusual character, or is he—just a man?"

The Italian shrugged his shoulders as he replied deprecatingly:

"My dear madam, just stop and think a moment. Isn't that a rather indiscreet question to put to a man—a man who is a friend of your husband—"

Hotly she turned on him.

"If you are his friend, why do you vilify and slander him behind his back?"

Keralio lifted up his long slender hands in pious protest.

"I vilify—my best friend— Oh, my dear Mrs. Traynor—you have quite misunderstood me. I am a foreigner. Perhaps it is that I express myself ill."

She shook her head skeptically. Firmly she said:

"No, Signor Keralio—you express yourself quite plainly. Now, I'll be equally frank with you. I confess there is one thing I do not understand. I have never understood it. I do not understand why my husband, a man so honorable, so straightforward in his dealings, a man so free from intrigue or reckless adventures, so regular, methodical and temperate in his habits, a man so entirely apart from the reckless, immoral kind of life you hint at, should have made a friend of *you*—"

The Italian raised his eyebrows, but there was only an amused smile on his bloodless lips as he said with a mock bow:

"Thank you, madam. You are very flattering."

"No—I mean it. I don't want to seem unkind, but your temperament and my husband's are as wide apart as the poles."

He opened wide his eyes as he asked,

"In what particular, *s'il vous plaît*?"

"Kenneth is frank, outspoken. He is not the type of man who takes rash risks. He is very conservative, scrupulously honest. He has fine ideals. While you—"

He laughed loudly.

"I? I am secretive, cunning, reckless, materialistic—is that it, madam?"

"I did not say so, but since you draw your portrait so well—"

He bit his lip. This girl with the flaxen hair and large lustrous eyes was more than a match for him in a battle of wits. He was making no headway at all. It was time to play his trump card. Softly he said:

"You said your husband was judicious, conservative—"

"So he is."

"That is a matter of opinion. Some might think otherwise. Of course, it is difficult for a woman when she is blinded by love—"

"What do you mean?"

"I mean that your husband is far from being the conservative, afraid-to-take-risks type of man you picture him. You women think you know your husbands. You know only such part of them as they themselves care to reveal. Perhaps if you knew to what extent your husband was involved in Wall Street, it would surprise you! Oh, everything is perfectly regular, of course. As treasurer of the Americo-African Mining Company, he has at his disposal large sums of money. He is also trustee of several large and valuable estates. All of this money he is supposed to invest—conservatively. He certainly invests it. Whether conservatively or not, I leave others to judge."

"Do you mean that he is using other people's money in Wall Street?"

"I mean, my dear lady, that he has the get-rich-quick fever. He has a rage for stock gambling—he is already heavily involved. I have often warned him to go slower, to be more prudent, but he won't heed my counsel. You know, he is very headstrong—your husband. As long as everything goes well he is all right. If anything goes wrong, he might find himself in an unpleasant predicament. Hasn't he spoken to you of these matters? Why should he worry you? It is as I told you. Husbands don't tell their wives everything—God forbid!"

Helen raised her hand. There was the ring of scorn in her voice as she exclaimed:

"Don't blaspheme, Signor Keralio. It sounds incongruous to hear the name of the Almighty on the lips of a man of your opinions and tastes. You think you live, but you don't. You go through life, seeking only to gratify your appetites, attracted only by material sensual pleasures. You ignore the best part of life—the pursuit of an ideal, a noble ambition, unselfishness, self-sacrifice. Really, Signor, I pity you—with all my heart."

He made no answer, but sat in silence watching her. Presently he said:

"Mrs. Traynor—do you know that you are an extraordinary woman?"

"In what way?" she demanded, elevating her eyebrows in surprise.

"You are either the cleverest or the most unsophisticated woman I have ever met. You are attractive enough to send a saint to perdition, yet you are quite indifferent to the power of your beauty and the tumult it arouses in the men who chance to cross your path. You seem to be absolutely without feeling. Yet I don't believe you devoid of temperament. I think I know women. I have met a good many. You do not belong to the type of cold, passionless women."

Again his eyes sought hers and found them. Again she tried to avoid his gaze and could not. There was something in his manner, his gestures, the tone of his voice, that conveyed to her more his real meaning than his actual words, yet, to her surprise, she was not aroused to anger. Sure of herself, she found herself listening, wondering what he would say next, ready to flee at the first warning of peril, but playing a dangerous game like the moth in the flame. As she sat back on the sofa, her head in the sofa cushions, he leaned nearer to her, and in those low, musical tones which held her under a kind of spell, he murmured:

"You are the cleverest woman I ever met."

She smiled in spite of herself, and he, mistaking the motive, thought she intended it as an encouragement. He glanced round to see if anyone was watching them, but Mr. Parker was peacefully dozing in a deep armchair a dozen yards away, and at the far end of the room Ray, Steell and Reynolds were engrossed in an exciting game of cards. Leaning quickly over, he seized her hand. His voice vibrating with passion, he said:

"Not only the cleverest, but the most desirable of women. Don't you see that you've set me afire? I'm mad for you! Helen—I want you!"

For a moment she was too stunned by his insolent daring to withdraw her hand, which he continued to press in his. His eyes flashing, he went on:

"Haven't you seen all along that I love you—desperately, passionately. You've set me afire. I'm mad for you. Let me awaken that love that's in your breast, but which your husband has never awakened. Let me—"

He did not finish, for that moment a small, jeweled hand,

Arthur Hornblow

suddenly torn from his grasp, struck him full on the mouth. Rising and trying with difficulty to control the emotion in her voice, she said quickly:

"You'd better go now—so as to prevent a scandal. If they knew, it might be awkward for you. Of course, you must never come here again."

That was all. She swept away from him with the dignity of an offended queen. The silence was deadly. All one heard was the silk rustle of her gown as she moved across the floor.

"It's my say," exclaimed Ray.

"I lead with trumps," said Steell.

"Signor Keralio has to go. Isn't it too bad!"

Mr. Steell and Dick rose and bowed politely.

There was nothing to be done. He was ignominiously dismissed like a lackey caught pilfering. But there was black wrath in his heart as he picked himself up, and turning to the others, he bowed and said:

"Good night."

CHAPTER VII

Dawn broke over the desert region of the Kalihari. The gray mists of the South African night slowly dissolved on the approach of the rising sun, until the crimson glow of the coming day, spreading high in the eastern heavens, tipped with gold the snow-clad peaks of the Drachenberg, and then, swiftly inundating the valley like a flood, chased away the shadows and filled the undulating plains with warmth and light.

Stretched out near the flickering embers of an expiring camp fire, not half a day's *trek* from the Vaal River, lay what, at first view, appeared to be bundles of rags. A closer inspection showed them to be the prostrate forms of two men, asleep. Huddled close together, as if seeking all possible protection from the keen air of the open *veldt*, they appeared grateful even for the little warmth that still came from the dying fire. Every now and again a tiny flame, bursting from one of the smouldering logs, would light up the recumbent figures, revealing a brief glimpse of the sleepers.

Both bore traces of desperate need. The rags they wore were filthy, and gave only scant protection from the weather, their emaciated faces and hollowed cheeks told eloquently of many days of fatigue and hunger; their feet, long since without shoes, were clumsily protected from the rocky *veldt* by pieces of coarse sacking. For weeks they had tramped across the great, merciless desert, guided only by the stars, often losing the trail, begging their way from farm to farm, glad to do little jobs for friendly Boers in return for a meal, always in peril of attack by

          Arthur Hornblow

hostile Kaffirs, yet never halting, trudging ever onward in their anxiety to reach the coast. That was the haven they painfully sought—the open sea where at least there was a chance to die among their fellows and not perish miserably like dogs on the lonely. God-forsaken plains, with only the howling jackal and the screaming vulture to pick their bones.

They had tried and they had lost in the great gamble. Like thousands of other reckless adventurers attracted to the newly discovered diamond country, they had rushed out there from England, confident that they, too, could wrest from nature that wonderful gem, ever associated with tragedy and romance, mystery and crime, for the possession of which, since history began, men have been ready to give up their lives. Confident of their success, they had risked all on a turn of the wheel, and Fortune, mocking their puny efforts, had first ruined and then degraded them, afterward sending them back home to die.

It was now quite light. The fire, which had flickered up fitfully at intervals, was entirely extinguished. A chilly wind had started to blow from the plateau on the north. The strangers stirred uneasily in their sleep and awoke almost simultaneously. Sitting up with a start, they yawned and rubbed their eyes.

"What show o' gettin' some breakfast, Handsome?" asked the smaller of the two.

"Damned little!" was the profane and laconic rejoinder.

They were men still in the early thirties. One was short and stocky, his face slightly pock-marked. Pictures of a mermaid and anchor clumsily tattooed in indigo on his wrist showed him to be a sailor. In fact, Dick Hickey, boatswain on *H. H. S. Tartar*, having taken French leave of his ship, as she lay in Cape Town Harbor, ran a very good chance of being taken back to England in irons as a deserter. Just now he was serenely indifferent as to what happened to him. Half dead from exposure and lack of nourishment, he would have gladly welcomed ship's officers or anybody else so long as there was some relief from his present sufferings. Meantime he spent what little breath he had left in cursing his hard luck, and blaming his companion as being solely responsible for his misfortune.

The latter was some few years his senior, stalwart and clean-limbed. He appeared to be over six feet in height and a man of splendid physique. At first glance it was evident that he came of superior stock. His shapely hands were grimy, his eyes of a peculiarly light shade of blue were hollow and haggard looking. His face, emaciated and ghastly, was almost livid. A clean-cut chin was covered with several weeks' growth of beard. Yet, underneath all these repellant externals, there was in his every attitude that indefinable refinement of manner which the world always associates with a gentleman. His dark hair, disheveled and matted, was unusually thick and bushy, with the exception of one spot, in the center of his forehead, where there was a single white lock, a capillary phenomenon, which imparted at once to his face from its very unusualness an individuality quite its own.

No one knew who he was or where he came from. They called him "Handsome Jack," partly because of his good looks and also on account of his reckless liberality with his cronies when flush. What his real name was no one knew or cared. It was a time when no one asked questions. As soon as the news of the astonishing diamond discoveries reached Europe, men began to flock to South Africa. Adventurers from all over the world gathered in Cape Town, a motley crew of incompetents and blacklegs, an investigation into the antecedents of any of whom was apt to have unpleasant results. That he was a professional gambler, he made no attempt to conceal, and that he had knocked about the world a good deal was also to be inferred from his wide knowledge of men and places. A man of aggressive, domineering personality, he was not without a certain following, attracted by his skill with cards and dice, but he was more feared than liked, and his reputation as a dangerous gunman kept inquisitive strangers at a safe distance. He was well known in every den frequented by the criminal and vicious, and it was in one of these resorts that Hickey had met him. The sailor had lost all his savings at faro. Dead broke, he was ready for anything which promised to recoup his fortunes. Handsome Jack laid before him a scheme which would make them both rich beyond the dreams of avarice. The recent discoveries on the Vaal had startled the world. A native had picked up a stone weighing over 80 carats. They might be equally lucky. All that was needed was pluck and patience. The plan was to make their way as best they could to the Vaal fields, jump a claim, and dig for diamonds.

They set out secretly, avoiding the larger caravans, making the long trek across the great plateau, partly by ox wagon, partly on foot. The trail led through a wild, desolate country, and gradually they left civilization hundreds of miles behind them. As far as the eye could reach in every direction was a monotonous desert of stone and sand, broken every now and then by small kopjies, the sides and summits of which were sparsely covered with thick brush and coarse grass. Scattered here and there, some twenty miles apart, were the homesteads of the Boer farmers and the thatched kraals of the dark-skinned Kaffirs. Over this lonely waste sheep and cattle wandered undisturbed by springbok, ostriches, crocodiles, mountain lions and other wild animals.

In this barren spot Nature had concealed her treasures. A child's cry of joy over a pretty pebble led to their discovery. The little son of a Boer farmer was playing one day in the fields near the homestead when his eye was attracted by something glittering at his feet. Stooping, he picked up a stone unlike any other he had ever seen. Interested, he began to look for others and found a number of them, which with great glee he carried home to show his mother. The worthy woman paid little heed to what, in her ignorance, she regarded merely as pretty stones, but she happened to speak about them to a neighboring farmer, who asked to look at them. Already tired of his new plaything, the child had thrown the stones away, but one was found in the field close by, and the neighbor, a shrewd Dutchman, who had heard of certain stones picked up in that locality having a certain value, offered to buy it. The good woman laughed at the idea of selling a stone, and made him a present of it. The farmer took it to the nearest town, where experts declared it to be a twenty-one carat diamond, worth $2,500. Round the world the telegraph flashed this remarkable story, and the rush to South Africa began. That was in 1870. In May of that year there were about a hundred men at the diggings in the Vaal fields. Before the next month had closed there were seven hundred. By April of the following year five thousand men were digging frantically in the mud along the Vaal and Orange rivers.

It was a rough, lawless gathering of men of every nationality under the sun, the criminal and the vicious, the idle and the worthless. The region being inside the border lines of the waste territory that lay between the Boers and the Hottentots, it was therefore No Man's Land, and beyond the pale of established law and order. The miners, compelled, in self-protection, to institute laws of their own, appointed committees to issue licenses, keep the peace, and punish offenders. Natives were whipped; white men were banished, and from this rough-and-ready justice there was no appeal.

When Handsome and Hickey arrived at the diggings, the fever was still at its height, and having secured a claim, they went to work with a will. Claims were thirty feet square, and to prevent speculation in them the owner, in order to hold title, was compelled to toil incessantly. It was hard work, harder work than Handsome had ever been put to in all his life. At the end of a few days, the skin was scraped off his hands from shoveling, and he had such a kink in his back that he couldn't straighten up. But he had come to stay, and a little; discomfort was not going to scare him. Their implements, purchased at the diggings, consisted of pick, shovel and rocker, this last being a box arranged on rockers like a baby's cradle. It was a clumsy yet useful contrivance, in which were fastened, one above the other, wire screens of varying fineness, the coarsest being on top. As Handsome dug the yellow earth out of the hole he shoveled it into the top screen. When it was full

Hickey poured in water while he rocked. The water washed the dirt through the holes, leaving the stones. These were taken out, emptied onto a sorting table, where Handsome scraped off the worthless peddles [Transcriber's note: pebbles?], saving anything that seemed of value. As a rule, and much to Hickey's disgust, the table was scraped clean. Sometimes the sailor would make a joyful exclamation on seeing some glittering pieces of rock crystal, thinking he had found a prize, only to be disappointed a moment later when a more experienced miner assured him it was worthless. Both soon learned, however, to recognize at sight the precious gems, and, although few came their way, they saw many brought to the surface by luckier neighbors. One day sounds of great rejoicing was heard in their tent. They had worked hard for over a month without finding anything, and were feeling greatly discouraged and dejected, when all at once something happened. Handsome had been rocking the cradle in a listless sort of way, and Hickey was sorting the residue, when suddenly the sailor gave a wild whoop of delight. Darting forward, he held up a glittering stone. Examination proved it to be a genuine diamond, weighing about ten carats, and valued at about $1,000. It was not much of a find, but it was enough to turn their heads. Dropping all work, they both proceeded to have "a good time," going on a drunken orgie, which lasted just as long as the money held out. When they came to their senses they were worse off than before. Weakened by prolonged debauch, they were in no mood for digging, and to complicate matters some one had jumped their claim during their absence. Even their tools had disappeared. Without resource or credit, they could not procure others. Yet work they must to keep the wolf from the door, so, cursing others when they had only themselves to blame, Handsome secured employment, digging for another miner, while the sailor performed such occasional odd jobs as he could pick up.

Broken in spirit, enraged at the long spell of ill luck, Handsome began to drink heavily. Every cent he made went to the grog shop, and Hickey, never over fond of work at any time, was only too glad of an excuse to drink with him. The two cronies filled themselves with rum until their reason tottered, and they became beasts, refusing to work, growing ugly, even menacing, preferring to beg the food their empty stomachs craved for rather than toil, as before. At last they made themselves such a nuisance that the attention of the vigilance committee was called to their particular case. In short order they were hauled up and ordered to leave camp. There was no alternative but to obey, and thus began the dreary trek homeward of the two broken and miserable outcasts.

"We cawn't go on much longer like this," moaned Hickey.

He made a painful effort to get up, but his joints, stiff from the all-night exposure, refused to obey his will, and he fell back with a groan. Handsome, more successful, had already risen, and was scanning the horizon on every side. Except for the kopjies, which in places obstructed the view, there was a clear range for ten miles or more. If anything alive moved within the field of vision, they could not help seeing it, but nothing greeted their eyes. There was neither man or beast to be seen; seemingly they were still many weary miles from the nearest homestead.

"We must go on," replied Handsome determinedly. Impatiently he added: "What do you want to do—stay here and let the jackals gnaw your bones?"

Hickey, too weak to argue, shook his head despondently.

"You go on, Handsome. Leave me here. I cawn't go any further, s' help me Gawd! My feet hurt somethin' awful. I'm all in. If ye get 'ome safe, go and see the old folks, will ye, and tell 'em I put up a good fight?"

"Hell!" retorted the other savagely. "Don't squat there crying like a baby. Be a man. Get up and let's hike it to the nearest homestead." Shading his eyes as he gazed earnestly over the plain, he added: "I see smoke in the distance. It can't be far off. Come—"

Suddenly, to his astonishment, Hickey leaped to his feet, with an agility unheard of in one so nearly dying. Pointing to the nearest kopjie, he shouted hoarsely:

"Look! There's a man—near that kopjie—he's coming this way!"

It was no dream. A man, unarmed and unaccompanied, was advancing toward them. From his dress and manner, it was easy to see that he was not a Boer farmer. He looked more like an Englishman or an American.

Scarcely able to believe the evidence of his own eyes, Handsome watched his progress.

As he came nearer, he waved his hand to show that he saw them, and he walked faster, as if afraid that they might disappear before he could reach them. Hickey, unable to restrain himself, had run forward, and in a few minutes they met.

"Who are you?" demanded the stranger, whose face, shaded as it was by a big canvas helmet, it was difficult to see.

"Miners from the Vaal," answered Hickey. "Who are you?"

"I am a Frenchman—Francois Chalat. I am ze valet of an American gentleman. Our party not know ze road. We has wandered from what you call ze trail. Will you show ze way to us?"

"Where's your party?" demanded Hickey.

Francois pointed to a kopjie about three miles distant.

"There! Behind zat hill."

Just at that moment, Handsome came lumbering up almost on the run, anxious to know what it was all about.

"Have you any whiskey?" was his first breathless ejaculation. "We're starving."

The valet made no answer. He was too startled to speak. Drawing back a few steps, he stared blankly at the big fellow. For several minutes he stood as if struck dumb. Presently, when he found his speech, he asked in awed tones:

"Who are you? What's your name?"

"What business is it of yours?" snapped Handsome, with some show of irritation. "Have you any food or whiskey? We're starving."

The valet made no answer, but just stared in astonished silence at the big six-footer who towered above him. For a moment he had thought it a trick that his master had played upon him. By walking quickly he had got there before him, and dressed up in these rags just to have fun with him. But that matted hair and that chin, with its weeks of growth of beard. He could not be deceived in that. No, this man was not his employer. Could it be possible, was it—his twin brother long since given up for dead? The same physique, the same features, the same eyes, the same thick, bushy hair with the single lock of white hair in the center of the forehead. There was no room for doubt. It was his employer's brother. It was just as well to make friends. Drawing a flask from his pocket and holding it out, he said:

"Here, take a drink. You need it."

Eagerly, Handsome snatched it out of his hand.

"You bet we do."

He took a deep gulp and handed it to Hickey, whose bleary eyes had watered at the very sight of the flask. Francois turned to Handsome.

"Where is ze trail?" he asked.

"Over yonder," growled the big fellow in surly tones and making a sweeping gesture with his arm which embraced every quarter of the compass.

"Rather indefinite, I should say," smiled the valet. "Where you go? Are you on ze way to ze mines?"

Handsome Jack took another pull at the flask. His good humor returning in proportion as he felt warmed up by the spirits, he said more amiably:

"I guess not. My pal and I have enough of the cursed place—ain't we, Hickey?"

The sailor man glanced dolefully at his limping foot, and nodded his head in acquiescence.

"You show us the trail home. My boss is very rich man," interrupted Francois quickly. "He pay anything."

Handsome pricked up his ears.

"Oh, he's rich, is he?"

The valet laughed as he replied:

"All Americans rich—tres riches. Did you ever hear of poor Americans?"

Hickey took another drink and snickered. Handsome looked thoughtful. After a pause, he said:

"What your boss' name?"

"Monsieur Traynor of the Americo-African Mining Co."

Handsome started.

"What? Kenneth Traynor, of the Americo-African Mining

Company—the people who made those sensational finds."

"Yes—he's vice-president of the company."

Handsome gave a low, expressive whistle.

"He's rich—all right! Do you know what those stones are worth?"

"Over a million dollairs."

"And he came out here to—"

The valet nodded.

"*Oui*—zat's it—to get ze big diamonds. We're on our way back from ze mines now. He has ze stones in his possession."

"And taking them to New York?" gasped Handsome; "a million dollars' worth?"

"Yes—taking zem to New York. That's what he came out for. We want to reach ze coast as soon as possible. Again I ask. Will you guide us back to ze trail?"

For a few moments Handsome made no answer. The thoughtful expression on his pale, care-worn face showed that he was thinking hard. What was passing in his mind no one knew, but whatever it was it caused the lines about his strong mouth to tighten and the steely blue eyes to flash. A million dollars? God! What will a man not do for a million dollars? Turning to the valet, he said hastily:

"Yes, I'm on. Take me to your party. I'll show you the trail. Quick, lead the way."

CHAPTER VIII

Traveling to and from the diamond fields in the days immediately following the first rush was not an unmixed joy. Express wagons drawn by eight horses or mules and running from Cape Town to Klipdrift once a week charged passengers sixty dollars a head, the journey across the plains taking about eight days. Travelers whose business was so urgent that they could not wait for the regular stage had to hire a team of their own at a much higher expense.

Kenneth did not mind the cost, if only he was able to make good time. The trip to the mines had been accomplished without mishap. Everything had gone as well as could be desired. He had been successful in securing valuable land options for the company, and at last the two precious stones were in his possession. That it was a big responsibility, he fully realized. The very knowledge that he had on his person gems worth over a million dollars, and this in a wild, uncivilized country where at any moment he might be followed, ambushed and killed, and no one the wiser, was not calculated to calm his nerves. But Kenneth Traynor had never known the meaning of the word fear. He was ready for any emergency and he went about unarmed, cool and unruffled. From his demeanor at least no one could guess that he ever gave a thought to the valuable consignment of which he was the guardian. Of course, it had been impossible to keep the thing secret. Everybody at the mines knew he had come out for the purpose of taking the big stones to America. Even his drivers knew, and so did Francois. The news was public property and was eagerly discussed over every camp fire as one of the sensations of the day. All this publicity did not tend to lessen the risk, and that was why he was so anxious to reach Cape Town without the least possible delay. He had timed his departure from the mines so as to just catch the steamer for England, and now, after all his trouble and careful calculation, the fool mule drivers had gone and lost the trail. It was most exasperating.

The wagon had come to a halt the night before under shelter of a fair-sized kopjie. The mules, tormented by the deadly *tetse* fly, stood whisking their tails and biting savagely at their hereditary enemy; the drivers, indifferent and stolid, sat on the ground smoking their pipes, while Kenneth, fuming at this unlooked for mishap which threatened an even more serious delay, strode up and down the *veldt*, swearing at the mules, the stolid drivers and everything else in sight.

Francois, who had left camp for assistance long before sunrise, had not yet returned. Unless help came soon they'd be held there another night. There was no use trying to proceed without a guide, for they might find themselves going round and round in a circle. There was nothing to do but wait until help came.

Sitting down on the stump of a tree near the fire, he tried to possess his soul in patience while one of the teamsters, who also officiated as cook, busied himself getting breakfast. It was now broad daylight; the weather clear and cold. As he sat there idly and smoked reflectively, his thoughts wandered home-ward, four thousand miles across the seas. He wondered what Helen was doing, if little Dorothy was well, if everything was all right. Only now he realized what the word home meant to him, and a chill ran through him as he thought of all the things that could happen. Yet how foolish it was to worry. What could happen? Helen had her sister constantly with her, and she was well looked after by Mr. Parker and Wilbur Steell. It was absurd to have any anxiety on that score. Besides, if anything had gone wrong, they would certainly have called him. He had had several letters from Helen, all of them saying she and baby were well and waiting eagerly for his return. Yes, he would soon be home now. In another two days he would reach Cape Town. From there to Southampton was only a fortnight's sail, and in another week he would be in New York.

These and kindred thoughts of home ran through his mind as he sat before the camp fire and tranquilly smoked his pipe. The drivers were busying themselves cleaning the harness, the mules were docilely browsing, the air was filled by a fragrant odor of coffee. His memories went back to his boyhood days. He recalled what the old nurse had told him about a twin brother. How strange it would be if he ever turned up. Such things were possible, of course, but hardly probable. No, the chances were that he was dead. If he had lived, how different everything might have been. He would have inherited half their father's money. What had been enough to start one so well in life would only have been a meagre provision for two. Yet it might have been an advantage, forced him to still greater effort. He might have got even farther than he had—who knows?

At that moment his reflections were interrupted by the sound of voices in the distance. He heard some one running. One of the teamsters came up hurriedly and exclaimed breathlessly:

"He's found some one, sir; he's got two men with him. They're coming now."

Kenneth jumped up and, shading his eyes, looked out across the yellow waste of stones and gravel. About a mile away he saw Francois, accompanied by two strangers, who looked like miners. They were tattered and miserable looking, as if down on their luck. One of them was limping as if lame; the other, much taller, although ragged and forlorn, had a soldierly bearing and the appearance of a gentleman. The valet, who had been walking faster than his companions, came up at that instant.

"Who have you got there?" demanded Kenneth.

"Two miners, monsieur. I found zem several miles away on ze *veldt*. They have tramped for days without food; they are starving."

"Do they know the trail?"

"Yes, monsieur. Ze big man knows ze trail. He will show ze way—for a consideration."

"Good! First give them some breakfast and then we'll go."

He waved his hand in the direction of the cook's mess, where the coffee was already steaming on the fire, and, turning away, began to gather his things together, preparatory to departure. There was no reason why he should have anything to say to the strangers. In fact, it would be better if they did not see him, or know who he was. It was possible that they had been at the mines when he arrived, in which case they would instantly recognize him as the American who had come to take the big diamonds to New York. Besides, they were not particularly attractive objects. What did their adventures and mishaps matter to him? He had troubles of his own. Francois could look after their wants. The main thing was to find the trail and get started back toward Cape Town as soon as possible. When the strangers had been fed they would set out, and, the trail once found, he would give them a lift on their way and a few sovereigns into the bargain. That would more than compensate them for all their trouble.

Meanwhile he thought he would take a quiet walk. His legs were stiff from sitting so long. A little exercise would do him the world of good. So, without a word to anybody, he slipped out of camp unobserved and started off at a brisk gait.

The region where they had halted seemed to be the center of Nowhere, a land where had reigned for all time the abomination of desolation spoken of by all the prophets. Knocking

Arthur Hornblow

about the world, as he had done for a lifetime, Kenneth had seen some queer spots in the world, but never had he come across so savagely repellent a spot as this. It was Nature in her harshest mood—not a vestige in any direction of human or animal life. There was not a farm, not a Boer or Kaffir, not even a tree to be seen. Nothing in every direction but a monotonous waste of yellow sand, rough stones and stunted grass. An unnatural stillness filled the air, making the silence oppressive, and uncanny. The soil was so poor that cultivation was impossible. The ground, strewn with broken rocks and sharp stones which cut the shoes and hurt the feet, suggested that in prehistoric times the plateau had been swept by a volcanic tempest. The slopes of the few scattered kopjies were sparsely covered with verdure and as he strode along, he passed here and there clumps of trees, veritable oases in the desert, or deep water holes under overhanging rocks where under cover of night, strange beasts came to drink. Apart from these few oases, it was a dreary monotonous waste of rock and sand, where neither beast or man could find food or shelter.

He had walked about three miles and was just passing a kopjie where a group of stunted trees offered a little shelter from the glare of the sun on the yellow gravel when he began to feel tired. Sitting down on a decayed tree stump, he took out his pipe, removed his helmet, and laying lazily back, closed his eyes, a favorite trick of his when he wished to concentrate his thoughts.

The trip, tiresome as it was, had certainly been worth while. His ambitious dreams had been more than realized. He could scarcely wait for his arrival to tell Helen the good news. He had secured signatures to a plan of consolidation of practically all the mining companies operating in South Africa. Until now, these companies had been engaged in a fierce and disastrous competition, which cut into each other's profits and cheapened the market price of stones. He had suggested a scheme of amalgamation which would put all the mines under one management, and fix arbitrary prices for diamonds which henceforth could not be sold under a certain figure agreed upon by the Syndicate. This plan, which had the general approval of the mining companies, practically gave Kenneth Traynor control of the diamond industry of the world, an industry which in South Africa alone had already produced 100,000,000 carats estimated to be worth $750,000,000. Overnight, Kenneth found himself many times a millionaire.

It had come at last—what he waited for all these years. This new consolidation deal meant great wealth to its promoters. What would he do with it? Most men need only enough for their actual needs, but he had higher aims. An ardent socialist he would use his money for the cause. Not, however, in the way others did, but to buy influence, power. He would fight Capitalism, in his own way. He would go into politics, run for public office, try and remedy some of the economic abuses from which people of the United States were now suffering. He would wage warfare on the high cost of living, on Greed and Graft. He would attack the Plutocracy in its stronghold, lay bare the inner workings of the System, the concentration of the wealth of the entire country in the hands of a few, by which the rich each year were becoming richer and the poor each year poorer. It would not be the first time a multi-millionaire had espoused the cause of the proletariat, but he would carry on the fight more vigorously than anyone had done. He would force an issue, make Greed disgorge its ill-gotten gains and accord to Labor its rightful place in the sun, its proper share of the world's production of wealth. His sympathies in the bitter struggle between the capitalists and the wage earners were wholly with the people who under the present wage system, had little chance to raise themselves from the mire. But he was intelligent enough to realize that the faults were not all on the side of Capital. Labor, too, needed the curb at times. Too ready to listen to the reckless harangues of irresponsible professional demagogues, wage earners were often as tyrannical as capitalists, insisting on impossible demands, rejecting sober compromise which, in the end, must be the basis of all amicable relations between employer and employed.

For some time he sat there, giving free rein to his imagination, when suddenly he fancied he heard the sound of heavy footsteps crunching on the hard sand. Raising his head he looked quickly round but seeing no one, concluded he was mistaken. Looking at his watch, he was amazed to find that he had been away from camp a whole hour. There was no time to be lost. The men had certainly finished eating by now; they could start at once. Jumping up he turned round to retrace his steps the same way he had come, when, suddenly, a shadow fell between him and the white road. Looking up, he was startled to see himself reflected as in a mirror against the green background of the kopjie.

At first he thought he must be ill. The walk, the sun, the exposure had no doubt overstimulated him and made him excited and feverish. He was seeing things. His success with the diamond deal had affected his brain. Of course, it was only an hallucination. The next time he looked this fantastic creation of his disordered mind would be gone. Again he glanced up in the direction of the kopjie. The apparition was still there, a horrible, monstrous, distortion of himself, standing still, speechless, staring at him. That it was only a mirage there could be no doubt. He had heard of such mirages at sea and also in the Sahara where wandering Arabs have beheld long caravans journeying in the skies. But he had never heard of a mirage lasting as long as this one. Would it never disappear? It must be a nightmare which still obsessed him. That was it. He had fallen asleep on the tree and was not yet awake. With an effort he made a step forward and tried to articulate, but the words stuck in his throat. Suddenly the spell was broken by the apparition itself, which moved and spoke. He recognized who it was now—one of the strangers brought in by Francois—but that astonishing likeness of himself—

Judging by the astonished expression on his face, Handsome was just as much surprised as Kenneth at the encounter. After satisfying his hunger he, too, had strayed away from the camp, unable to control his impatience while the teamsters were harnessing the mule team. He had left Hickey to gorge still more while he strutted on by himself, cogitating on what the valet had told him in regard to the diamonds. This sudden meeting with the very man who had been uppermost in his thoughts was surprising enough, and instantly he, also, was struck with the extraordinary resemblance between them.

"Who the devil are you?" he demanded in surly tones.

Thus rudely aroused to the reality, and seeing that it was really a creature of flesh and blood he had to deal with and not a creature of another world, Kenneth answered haughtily:

"I'm not accustomed to being addressed in that manner."

Handsome laughed mockingly. With affected politeness he retorted:

"Your lordship's servant! What is his lordship's pleasure?"

Kenneth did not hear the taunting reply or heed the sneer. He was still staring at this counterpart of himself, this very image yet who was not himself, but a human derelict, a wretched, sodden outcast. All at once, an overwhelming, horrible suggestion rushed across his brain. Could it be, was it—his long lost twin brother? Almost gasping, he demanded:

"Who are you?"

Handsome chuckled.

"I don't know."

"What is your name?"

The man chuckled.

"They call me Handsome. That's because I'm a good looker. I have had a good many other names, but I've forgotten what they are. The police know. It's all in the records."

"My God—a police record!"

"What of it?" Bitterly he added: "We can't all be fine gentlemen and millionaires."

"Where are you from?"

"Nowhere."

"Who were your parents?"

"Never had any that I know of."

Kenneth started forward and, seizing the man's left hand, closely examined it. Yes, there was the scar on the index finger of the left hand. No further doubt was possible. This was his brother. Handsome, meantime, had been watching the other's agitation with mingled interest and amusement.

Hoarsely, Kenneth cried:

"Where have you been all these years?"

Handsome stared as if he thought his interlocutor had gone crazy. Almost angrily he retorted:

"What d—d business is it of yours?"

Paying no heed to the miner's offensive attitude, and anxious only to learn something of his history, Kenneth approached him and held out his hand.

"I wish to be your friend."

Handsome drew back suspiciously. Always associated with evil himself, he looked for only evil from others. Bitterly he retorted:

"My friend—what do your kind care for poor devils like me?"

For answer, Kenneth removed his helmet, suddenly revealing the solitary lock of white hair. Handsome fell back in surprise. For the first time he realized the extraordinary resemblance. He had noticed a marked likeness before, but now the diamond promoter's helmet was off, it was positively startling. Hoarsely he exclaimed:

"The devil! Who are you? You look just like—"

Kenneth looked at him keenly for a moment. Then he said calmly:

"Yes—I look just like you. No wonder. You are—my brother!"

"Your brother?"

"Yes—my brother. We are twins. You were kidnapped by gypsies thirty-two years ago. Our old nurse told me the story for the first time the day before I sailed from New York. She also told me about that scar on your hand. You cut it badly when you were a year old and the scar has remained ever since. Everybody believed you dead. Where have you been all these years?"

Handsome made no answer but fell back a few steps, and passed his hand over his brow as if bewildered. This astonishing revelation had been made so suddenly that it had left him dazed. A wild, improbable tale, it seemed, yet perhaps there was some truth in it. He had never known who his parents were and it had always seemed to him that he came of better stock than those with whom he associated. Then again, there was the ridiculous likeness. One had only to look at them both—it was the same face.

Slowly, gradually, as he looked more closely at Kenneth the conviction grew stronger that this, indeed, was his brother, his own flesh and blood, yet it aroused within him no emotion and left him entirely cold. No impulse seized him to throw himself into this man's arms and embrace him. His heart was

Arthur Hornblow

steeled against the world. Human affection and sympathy had dried up in his breast years ago. What he saw was not a kinsman, a brother, but a man who had succeeded in life where he had failed, a man who was rich and happy while he was poor and miserable, a man who had everything while he had nothing. And if the tale were true, if indeed, he were this rich man's brother, it only made matters worse, for he had been robbed of his rightful inheritance. This rich man was enjoying wealth half of which rightfully belonged to him.

Again Kenneth demanded:

"Where have you been all these years?"

"Here, there, everywhere," was the sullen answer. "London, Paris, Brussels, Vienna, New York, Boston, Chicago, Havana, Buenos Ayres. I know them all and they know me—perhaps too well. My earliest recollection is of the Italian quarter in New York, a long narrow always dirty street, bordered on either side by dilapidated greasy tenements, ricketty fire escapes filled with biddy and garbage. Pietro lived there and kept his organ in the basement cellar. When Pietro went out with the organ he took me along to excite sympathy. Until I was fifteen years old I begged to support Pietro. One day he beat me and I ran away and shipped as cabin boy on a sailing vessel bound for Liverpool. I reached London and found employment as stable boy at Ascot. There I learned the fatal fascination of gambling. With what I saved from my wages I bet on the horses. I won and won again. I went back to London and frequented the gambling houses. I won, always won. One day there was a row. Someone complained I had cheated. The police arrested me. When I left jail I went to the continent and began gambling again. I have gambled ever since." Pointing in the direction of the mines he added bitterly:

"That was my last gamble and I lost. That's all I have to tell."

Kenneth listened with keen interest. When the other stopped

speaking he asked:

"And now—what will you do?"

Handsome shrugged his shoulders and made no answer. Kenneth went on:

"You can't keep up the old life—that is impossible. You owe something to the blood that's running in your veins. There is only one thing for you to do. You must break off with the past for good, and come home with me. Are you known in New York?"

Handsome shook his head.

"No, I never returned there since I was a child."

"Your operations in America were confined to San Francisco, Chicago and St. Louis—"

"Yes."

Kenneth breathed more freely.

"That makes matters easier. No one in New York, therefore, has anything against you. There it will be possible to live down your past. You will cease being an outcast, a wanderer on the face of the earth. You will take the place in society for which Nature intended you."

Handsome smiled cynically. Grimly he replied:

"I guess Nature never expected much of me."

"You never can tell," said Kenneth quickly. "Your environments no doubt were responsible for your downfall. You have been a victim of circumstances."

Handsome was silent. This free roving life had come second

nature to him. He looked with suspicion on any other. After a pause, he asked:

"What can I do in New York?"

"I will dress and house you like a gentleman. For a time you can make your home with us. If we find we can't agree, well— we'll part. I will find you employment—"

Handsome laughed. Mockingly he said:

"Then I am to be dependent on you—"

"No—not on me—. On your own efforts. There is no reason why, if given a chance, you will not make a success in the world. You are still young and energetic. I will give you a start in any line you wish to enter. I will make you a present of $10,000. It should be enough capital to start in any business."

Handsome shrugged his shoulders.

"Charity?" he exclaimed.

"No—not charity—brotherly affection."

His brother laughed mockingly. Bitterly he exclaimed:

"Maybe it's conscience money."

"What do you mean?"

"You inherited from our father, didn't you?"

"Yes—but I've increased it a hundred-fold by my own efforts."

"How much did he leave you?"

"Twenty thousand dollars."

"Why didn't he leave me some?"

"He believed you dead. The sum I offer you is the sum you would have inherited from our father had he known you were living. Do you accept?"

Handsome was silent. His brain was working fast. What this man offered him was the merest pittance. Put out at interest, it would give him the princely income of $10 a week. What did he care for the good opinion of the world? He had knocked about so long, roughing it everywhere, that he might as well end as he had begun—an adventurer. Suddenly there flashed across his brain a wild, audacious idea—a scheme so fantastic, so fraught with adventure and peril that the very thought gave him a thrill. It involved violence, possibly a crime. Well, what of it? He was not the kind to be deterred by trifles. This man was nothing to him. Brotherly love, family ties—these were simply phrases to one who had never known them. He knew and obeyed only one instinct—the fight for life, the survival of the fittest. Society had waged war on him; he would be merciless in his war on society. This man—this alleged brother, threw him a sop, insulted him by offering him charity. Why should he hesitate? It was his life or another's. There was a big prize to be won. Life was sweet when one has millions to enjoy it with. This man had now on his person diamonds worth over a million and he had more millions at home. Suppose something happened to this man here in South Africa and he went home in his stead to take his place in his household and enjoy his millions? Who would know the difference?

Impatient at the other's silence Kenneth demanded somewhat sharply:

"Well—what do you say? Do you accept?"

He looked straight at his *vis-a-vis*, but Handsome avoided his

Arthur Hornblow

direct gaze. He was silent for another moment as if reflecting. Then, slowly, he said:

"Yes, I accept."

CHAPTER IX

The string orchestra, adroitly concealed behind a bank of graceful exotic plants, struck up a languorous waltz, and the couples, only too eager to respond to the invitation, began to turn and glide over the polished parquet floor.

Not since its master's departure for South Africa had the Traynor residence been the scene of so much life and gayety. Every window literally blazed with light. From the front door at the top of the high stoop down to the edge of the street curb, stretched a canvas awning to protect arriving guests from the inclemency of the weather.

It was a stormy night. The rain was falling in torrents, but no one cared. Everybody was out for a good time and they knew that this was the house to get it.

Helen's first impulse had been to postpone the affair, held really in celebration of Ray's birthday, until Kenneth's return, but as this idea had met with decided opposition from the younger element, she had reluctantly given way. Besides, there was no knowing when Kenneth would return. Nothing as yet had been heard from him excepting a brief cablegram announcing his safe arrival at Cape Town, and it was manifestly unfair to let her own inclinations stand in the way of the happiness of others. So, after due reflection, she had surrendered completely, giving Ray *carte blanche* to make what arrangements she chose. That young person did not stand on the order of going. She acted at once and sent out invitations to what proved to be

Arthur Hornblow

one of the biggest *soirees dansantes* of the season. Everything was done on a most liberal scale. The house was decorated by Herly, three picturesque fiddlers were obtained from an agency, and Mazzoni, who provides delicacies for the "400," had charge of the catering.

Everybody who was anybody was invited, all Ray's personal friends besides a lot of people she did not know so well. A number of Helen's intimates were there and also some men friends of Mr. Steell and Dick Reynolds. The girls in their light gowns looked pretty as angels. The men were handsome, attentive and gallant. Altogether, everyone voted it one of the most enjoyable social affairs of the year.

Ray had danced her sixth waltz and at last utterly exhausted, unable to stand any more, she allowed Dick Reynolds to escort her to a sofa.

"Please get me an ice, will you? That's a dear boy," she gasped.

"Will I!" echoed the youth. "What wouldn't I do for you—fire and water—that's all!"

"As bad as that?" laughed the girl panting. "Please don't be silly. Go and get me an ice."

Obediently, he left her and forced his way through the throng to the buffet, while Ray, left alone, started to fan herself vigorously. As she sat there Helen passed on the arm of Mr. Parker. The President stopped short and quizzed the young girl.

"You here?" ejaculated the old gentleman in mock amazement. "Why aren't you dancing? This will never do."

Helen smiled.

"I expect she's tired out. This is the first time I've seen her sit down all evening."

Ray nodded.

"You've guessed right, sis. I'm nearly dead. I sent Dick for an ice."

"Did you ever see such a crowd?" remarked the president of the A. A. M. Company as he surveyed the throng that passed in and out of the rooms.

"Oh, Mrs. Traynor we're having such a jolly time," exclaimed a tall graceful girl, gracefully dressed in light blue empire gown with Grecian head dress.

"I'm so glad, dear," smiled the hostess amiably. Turning to Mr. Parker as the girl passed on she asked: "Do you know who that is?"

He shook his head.

"She's the granddaughter of John R. Rockerford, the money king. Fancy her saying this is jolly after the grandeur she is accustomed to!"

"No doubt she likes this better," retorted Ray. "Those very rich people don't do things any better than we—sometimes not so well. Their parties are too stiff and formal."

Suddenly Mr. Parker nudged his hostess.

"Here comes Mrs. Brewster-Curtis," he said in a stage whisper. "They say her husband's worth ten millions—all made from graft."

A handsome woman, blazing with diamonds, came up. Addressing Helen, she exclaimed gushingly:

"Oh, Mrs. Traynor, isn't this perfectly delightful? How do you do, Mr. Parker. Do you know I haven't enjoyed myself so much this season. What's the news from your dear husband?"

"No news as yet."

"Dear me—you poor thing! How interesting—so pretty and husband away. What an opportunity for some of our gay Lotharios!"

"They wouldn't have much chance with Helen!" laughed Ray.

Mrs. Brewster-Curtis turned, and putting up her gold lorgnon, stared at the unknown young woman who had been so bold to venture to express an opinion. Ray, meantime, was wondering what detained Dick. Here she was famishing with thirst and still no ice. Her partner had disappeared completely.

Addressing her hostess Mrs. Brewster said languidly:

"Your niece, I believe."

"No—my sister," corrected Helen with a smile. It was a mistake often made.

"Of course—of course, how silly of me. I might have known that. You look enough alike."

"Do you think so?" interrupted Ray hotly. "Helen is far prettier than I."

"You are no judge, my dear. You must let the men decide that."

"They do," said Ray, "and they all declare in favor of Helen."

"Not by the way Mr. Steell dodges [Transcriber's note: dogs?] your footsteps." Looking up she exclaimed: "There he is now."

"Oh, Mr. Steell," cried Helen, "don't forget our next waltz."

His face all smiles, the lawyer forced his way through the press of people.

"Have you seen Dick?" asked Ray. "I sent him to get me an ice."

Mr. Steell laughed outright.

"Oh, it was you who sent him. If I had known—"

"Why?" demanded Ray, opening wide her eyes. "Where is he? I want my ice."

"I'll get you an ice, dear," said Helen.

"No, let me go," exclaimed Mr. Parker.

"No—no one will get the ice but myself," said Mr. Steell. "It's my fault that the ice is not already forthcoming. It is only just that I suffer accordingly."

Mr. Parker laughed.

"The ice episode threatens to become a diplomatic incident."

"Why—whatever is the matter?" smiled Helen.

The lawyer was so much amused that he could hardly keep his face straight. With an effort he controlled himself, and said:

"Just now I was talking with a pretty girl and Dick suddenly forced his way through the crowd, going in the direction of the buffet. I had no idea on what a serious mission he was bound, of course, and so I called him to introduce him to the pretty girl, who had with her an aunt, a veritable witch, as hideous as a Medusa, and who, in addition, is afflicted with a wooden leg. Dick gave the aunt only a glance. That was enough, but he was all smiles for her pretty niece, who, I must admit, is somewhat of a flirt. Anyhow she rolled her eyes so eloquently at him that he forgot all about the important errand on which he was bound. Just at that moment the musicians struck up a *schottische*, and, on the spur of the moment, he asked the pretty girl to dance. She declined, with an arch smile, but, pointing to the old witch, said her aunt would be delighted. Poor Dick! There was no help for it. The Medusa got up, seized him in her claws, and, the last thing I saw of the poor youth, they were doing a sort of Bunny Hug, the wooden leg of his lady partner marking time on the waxed floor."

"Please stop! If you go on—I shall expire."

Ray was nearly in convulsions of laughter in which all joined. When Helen had somewhat regained her composure, she said:

"I think it's unkind to make fun of the poor woman. Who is she?"

"I haven't the least idea. Perhaps Dick will tell us."

At that moment the youth emerged from the throng and came towards them, his linen mussed, his hair dishevelled. But in one hand he held grimly a plate of ice cream. Looking shamelessly at Ray, he smiled:

"I've got it—at last."

"Where have you been all this time?" she demanded innocently.

"Oh, I've been having no end of a good time!"

Steell burst out laughing.

"Did she ask you to call, Dick?"

"If she had I'd have killed her."

"How did the artificial leg work?"

"She jammed it on my foot once. How it did hurt!"

Ray, by this time, was almost in hysterics, and Helen and the others, catching the contagion, the whole group were soon shaken by uncontrollable laughter.

The orchestra struck up a quadrille. A man came rushing up to Ray.

"My dance, I believe."

With a comical expression of resignation, the young girl allowed herself to be led away, while Helen and Mrs. Brewster-Curtis took seats to watch the figures.

"Come, Dick," said Steell in an undertone. "Let's go and smoke a cigar."

Leading the way he went into the smoking-room, where cigars and liquors were laid out. Turning to the youth, he inquired eagerly:

"Well—what about the Signor? What have you found out?"

Dick lit a cigarette and then calmly he said:

"Everything."

"What—to be specific."

"He's all and more than we expected."

"In other words—a crook?"

"Yes, and a dangerous one."

"What's his game?"

"Confidence man, bank robber, blackmailer."

"How did you find out?"

"Very easily. I found his record. The police haven't disturbed him because his clever disguise has deceived them. They have not recognized in the polished, suave Signor Keralio, the popular fencing master, the man they have been hunting for years. His real name is Richard Barton. His pals call him Baron Rapp. Five years ago he was convicted of robbing a bank out West and was sent up for ten years. He served a year in Joliet and then broke jail and he has been at liberty ever since."

"Good!" exclaimed the lawyer, rubbing his hands with satisfaction. "We've got him where we want him. What else?"

"He has managed to elude the police so far owing to the fact that he has not been operating of late, but from what I've been able to ferret out, he is preparing some big haul. Everything points that way. I don't know what it is, but it's the biggest thing in which he has yet been mixed up. He's affiliated with crooks who operate all over the country. Some of his men are disguised as servants and valets in rich houses. They spy on their masters and tell him if there is anything worth robbing. He is the master-mind that schemes the operations that others carry out. He tells his men what banks and homes to break into and instructs them how to do it. He receives all the stolen property. At this very moment his flat in the Bronx is full of stolen loot. I also suspect him of being engaged in counterfeiting."

The lawyer was lost in admiration.

"Dick, you're a wonder!"

The young man grinned with pride.

"Well—what's it to be—shall we tip off the police?"

"Not by a long shot. We'll have the gun loaded—all ready for use. If the Signor gets ugly we'll shoot—that's all. Not a word, do you hear. Leave everything to me. Come, let's go back or they'll think something's wrong."

In the ballroom, they were still dancing the quadrille, the pretty gowns of the girls and black coats of the men making a picturesque sight as they blended in the ever changing figures.

The gayety was at its height when the maid entered and whispered in her ear:

"There's a gentleman downstairs."

Helen looked at the girl in surprise.

"A gentleman? What's his name?"

"I don't know, m'm. He wouldn't say."

"Very well, I'll go down."

Slipping away unobserved, Helen made her way downstairs and throwing back the heavy tapestry portieres entered the drawing room which was almost in complete darkness. The maid had forgotten to switch on the electrolier and as the only light came from the distant dining-room, the big parlor was practically all in gloom. Before her eyes had become quite accustomed to the dark, a man advanced out of the shadow. It was Signor Keralio.

She recognized him instantly and instinctively she shrank back, alarmed. How had he dared come again to her house after what had occurred? He noticed the movement and asked:

"I see that I'm unwelcome. Do I frighten you so much?"

Coldly she answered:

"You do not frighten me. You surprise me. I did not expect this pleasure after what passed between us the last time you were here." Making a half turn, as if about to leave the room, she added quickly: "I have company upstairs. You must excuse me."

She walked away and had almost reached the door, when, with a quick stride, he intercepted her.

"Please don't go. I am here in your own interest. I want to talk to you—just a moment, about—"

She hesitated.

"About what?" she demanded haughtily.

"About your husband."

"My husband?" she echoed, turning and facing him.

"Yes—your husband. He is in danger. I want to help you and—him."

"Kenneth in danger?" she faltered. "What do you mean?"

He pointed to a chair.

"Won't you sit down. I won't keep you a moment. I will tell you everything—"

She sat down like one in a dream. Taking a seat near her, he began in his low, musical tones.

"Peril threatens your husband. It is known that he has gone to South Africa to bring home diamonds of almost inestimable value. A number of desperate men, who stop at nothing to accomplish their ends, have taken steps to secure the diamonds at any cost—even at the price of a human life."

A chill ran through her, but her voice was firm as she demanded scornfully:

"You know these men—these murderers?"

"Yes—I know them."

Instantly came the bitter retort:

"Maybe you are one of them!"

His eyes flashed in the darkness and his voice vibrated with passion as he answered:

"I know you think ill of me. You do me an injustice. I have no share in these men's operations, but I have great power over them. They must obey my command. They know that and so respect my orders. A word from me and your husband will be unmolested."

Like the drowning man who in his agony will grasp eagerly at a floating straw, Helen seized at the hope his words held out. That Kenneth was in peril she readily believed. It was a dangerous mission. She had scented danger from the outset. This man might be lying, and yet he might have the influence he boasted.

"You can avert the danger?"

He nodded.

"I can."

"How?"

"I will give orders that he be unmolested."

"And they will obey you?"

"They will."

Her face brightened. More amiably she said:

"You'll do this, won't you?"

"Yes—for a price."

"What price?"

"That you recall what you said the other day and restore me to a place in your friendship."

There was no mistaking his true meaning. It was a price no self-respecting woman could pay. She rose indignantly, and haughtily she said:

"You have never had a place in my friendship, Signor Keralio, and you never will. I see through your motive and I despise you now all the more. My husband, who is an honorable man, would be the first to have done with me forever if I entered into any such bargain. He has mistaken your character. When he returns I will enlighten him, and he will tell you himself that his wife has no dealings with a scoundrel. As for your threats, and tale of mysterious danger, I don't believe a word you say. But I may think it worth while to cable my husband in order to put him on his guard and to inform the police. Good night!"

Before he could stop her, she had touched an electric bell and left the room. The next instant Roberts, the butler, appeared and threw open the front door. There was nothing to do but go.

She had defied him.

CHAPTER X

Eagerly, breathlessly, Helen tore open the cablegram.

It was late Saturday afternoon and she had been with Ray and Mr. Steell to see some paintings—a private view of a remarkable collection of old masters. After having tea at the Plaza they had taken a brisk walk through the Park, the lawyer insisting that the exercise would do them good.

"It's just come, m'm," said the maid, holding out the thin envelope.

"Oh, it's from Kenneth!" exclaimed Ray excitedly, throwing down her muff and running to look over her sister's shoulder.

For long, dreary weeks Helen had expected, and waited for, this message, and now it had come, she was almost afraid to read it. There were only a few words, cold and formal, the usual matter-of-fact, businesslike phraseology of the so-much-a-word telegram:

> CAPE TOWN, Thursday (delay in transmission). Sail today on the *Abyssinia*. All's well. KEN.

"Is that all?" exclaimed Ray, disappointed.

Mr. Steell laughed.

"How much more do you expect at $2 a word?"

"Well, he might be a little more explicit," pouted Ray. "If I were his wife, that wouldn't satisfy me."

Helen laughed lightly. Her eyes sparkling, her usually pale cheeks filled with a ruddy color from her walk in the park, the lawyer thought he had never seen her looking so pretty.

"It satisfies me," she said, her face all lit up with joyous excitement. "All I want to know is that he is safe and on his way home. The cablegram is dated Thursday. Then he's already on the water three days! I wonder why we didn't hear before?"

Mr. Steell glanced over her shoulder.

"The dispatch has been delayed. Don't you see? It says, 'delayed in transmission.'"

Helen turned round, her face radiant.

"When ought he to get here?"

The lawyer was silent for a moment as if calculating. Then, looking up, he said:

"The *Abyssinia* is not a very fast boat. I suppose she is the best he could get. She's due at Southampton two weeks from to-day. A week after that, he ought to be in New York—providing nothing happens."

Helen, who was still reading and re-reading the cablegram, looked up quickly. With a note of alarm in her voice, she exclaimed:

"Providing nothing happens! What could happen?"

"Oh, nothing serious, of course. In these days of the wireless nothing ever happens to steamers. One is safer traveling on the sea than on land. I didn't mean anything serious, but merely that sometimes boats are delayed by bad weather or by fog. That prevents them arriving on schedule time."

Almost three months had slipped by since Kenneth's departure from New York. To Helen it had seemed so many years. She had tried to be contented and happy for Ray's sake. She entertained a good deal, giving dinner and theater parties, keeping open house, playing graciously the role of chatelaine in the absence of her lord, to all outward appearances as gay and light-hearted as ever. Only Ray and her immediate friends knew that the gayety was forced.

The poison had done its deadly work. The few words uttered by Signor Keralio that afternoon shortly after her husband's departure had burnt deep into her mind like letters of fire. Well she guessed the object of the wily Italian in speaking as he did. It availed him nothing, and she only despised him the more. It was cowardly, contemptible, and, from such a source, absolutely unworthy of belief. Yet secretly it worried her just the same. She had always considered Kenneth's life an open book. She thought she knew his every action, his every thought. The mere suggestion that her husband might have other interests, other attachments of which she knew nothing took her so by surprise that she was disarmed, powerless to answer. The innuendo that he might be unfaithful had gone through her heart like a knife. Of course it was quite ridiculous. He was not that kind of man. It was true he had often gone away on trips that seemed unnecessary, and now she came to think of it Kenneth's absences had of late been both frequent and mysterious. Then, too, she had no idea of the extent of his operations in Wall Street. She knew he bought and sold stocks sometimes. That is only what every investor does. But it was incredible that he was involved to the extent Keralio said he was. She knew he was ambitious to acquire wealth, but that he would take such fearful risks and jeopardize funds which, after all, belonged, not to him, but to the stockholders—that was impossible. It was a horrible libel.

Still another cause for worry was the health of her little

daughter, Dorothy. Nothing ailed the child particularly, but she was not well. The doctor said nothing was the matter, but a slight temperature persisted, together with a cough which, naturally, alarmed the young mother out of all proportion to the seriousness of the case. The doctor also advised a change of air, so Helen at once made arrangements to send her little daughter to Philadelphia, where, in Aunt Carrie's beautiful house, she would have the best air and attention in the world. Aunt Carrie came to New York to fetch the child, and, as she stayed a couple of weeks sight-seeing and visiting friends that also helped to keep Helen busy.

"I do wish that I didn't have such a worrying disposition"— she laughed nervously after the lawyer had been at some pains to assure her about the sea-worthiness of the *Abyssinia*. "Really, it makes me so unhappy, but I simply can't help it. The other day it was baby who made me terribly anxious; now it is Kenneth's home-coming. I must seem very foolish to you all."

Ray quickly protested.

"You sweet thing—how could you look foolish? What an idea! Only please don't worry, dear. I never do."

Mr. Steell nodded sympathetically.

"It's nothing to be ashamed of, Mrs. Traynor. It shows you have a fine, sensitive nature. It is only the grosser natures that are callous and unaffected by the anxieties of life."

Taking the remarks to herself, Ray threw up her head indignantly.

"I deny the imputation that I'm gross."

The lawyer laughed.

"You are far too healthy to worry. Moreover, you have nothing to worry about. If a man you loved were six thousand miles away—"

"Yes," interrupted Helen; "that's it. Only those who care for each other can understand—"

"Oh, of course!" retorted her sister, flaring up. "We spinsters, belonging, as we do, to the sisterhood of the Great Unloved, are quite incompetent to express an intelligent opinion on that or on any other matter. I grant that, but is Mr. Steell, a confirmed old bachelor, any more competent than I?"

"Hardly an old bachelor!" interrupted Helen reprovingly.

"No—middle-aged bachelor!" corrected Ray saucily. "He never cared for a woman in his life. He—"

"Who told you so?" inquired the lawyer quickly, with an amused twinkle in his eye.

Ray colored visibly.

"Oh, I judge so," she stammered. "You never speak of that sort of thing. One can only draw conclusions."

"The conclusions may be wrong," he replied gravely. "My life is a very busy one. I have had no time to think of anything outside my immediate work. Yet I am human. I sometimes yearn for the companionship of a good woman. A pretty face attracts me, as it does other men, but, in my opinion, any such attachment is too serious a matter to be treated lightly. When a man feels deeply he keeps his own confidence until the moment comes when he can unburden himself and say what is in his heart."

"I like that," said Helen, nodding her head approvingly.

Ray jumped up to conceal her embarrassment.

"Oh, how terribly serious you two are to-day!" she exclaimed.

"I declare I'll run away unless you cheer up a bit. Suppose I get some tea?"

"Excellent idea!" laughed the lawyer.

Ray touched a bell, and went to clear a small side table, which she drew up near where they were sitting.

"There!" she exclaimed, smiling roguishly at the lawyer. "Don't you think I'm smart?"

"Of course we do." Lowering his voice he added significantly: "At least I do."

Apparently the compliment fell on deaf ears, for, turning her head away, she said quickly:

"Please don't be sarcastic."

More seriously, and in the same tone, that even Helen, who was only a short distance away, could not hear, he said:

"I'm never sarcastic. I think you are all a woman should be."

"Do you mean that?"

"I do. I have thought it for a long time."

"Really?"

"Really."

The young girl colored with pleasure. For all her sophisticated and independent manner she was still a child at heart. She had no thoughts of marriage, but it flattered her to think that she had the power to attract and interest this serious, brilliant man of the world. She said nothing more, relapsing into a meditative silence as she busied herself helping the maid to set out the tea table.

To Helen it was a source of keen satisfaction to notice the attention which the brilliant young lawyer was paying her sister. She had long recognized his sterling qualities. He was a man of whom any woman might well be proud. He could not but make a good husband. Next to Kenneth and her baby no one was dearer to her than Ray and, since their mother died, she had felt a certain sense of responsibility. To see her well and happily married was the one secret wish of her life.

But overshadowing these preoccupations at present were those other new anxieties which preyed upon her sensitive mind with all the force of an obsession. Was there any part of her husband's life that he had hidden from her? Was he really as loyal as she had always fondly and blindly believed; had his ambition led him to take grave financial risks that might one day jeopardize their comfort and happiness, the very future of their child?

Ray rose to put away the tea table, and she found herself sitting alone with the lawyer. There was a moment's silence, and then, as if thinking out aloud what was on her mind, she said:

"Thank God, he's safe; I had the most fearful premonitions—"

The lawyer laughed.

"Don't put your trust in premonitions—things happen or they don't happen. It's absurd to believe that misfortunes are all prepared beforehand."

"Then you are not a fatalist?"

"Decidedly not. I hope I have too much intelligence to believe in anything so foolish."

"Do you believe in a Supreme Being who has the same power to suddenly snuff us out of existence as he had to create us?"

"I neither believe nor disbelieve. Frankly, I do not know. What

Arthur Hornblow

people call God, Jehovah, Nature, according to my reasoning, is an astounding energy, a marvellous chemical process, created and controlled by some unknown, stupendous first cause, the origin of which man may never understand. How should he? He has not time. We are rushed into the world without preparation. We are ignorant, helpless, blind. Gradually, by dint of much physical labor and mental toil, we succeed in ferreting out a few facts regarding ourselves and the physical laws that govern us. We are just on the verge of discovering more—we are just beginning to understand and enjoy life—when suddenly we find ourselves growing old and decrepit. Our physical and mental powers fail us, and the same force that benevolently created us now mercilessly destroys us, and we are hurled, willy-nilly, back into eternity whence we came. Rather absurd, isn't it?"

Intensely interested Helen looked up. Eagerly she exclaimed:

"You have a whole system of philosophy in a mere handful of words, haven't you?"

He smiled.

"It's all one needs, and perhaps as good as those more complicated and more verbose."

More seriously and lowering her voice so Ray, who was still busy at the other end of the room, might not overhear, she said:

"Mr. Steell—you are so clever—you know all about everything. Tell me, do you know anything about Wall Street?"

The ingenuousness of the question amused him. With a laugh he answered:

"A little—to my sorrow."

"It's a dangerous place, isn't it?"

"Very; it has a graveyard at one end, the East River at the other, two places highly convenient at times to those who play the game."

"If luck goes against him, a man could lose his all, then?"

"Not only his all but the all of others, too—if he's that kind of a man."

She was silent for a moment. Then she continued:

"And sometimes even fine, honest men are tempted, are they not, to gamble with money which is not theirs?"

"Many have done so. The prisons are full of them. There is nothing so dangerous as the get-rich-quick fever. All the men who gamble in stocks have it. It becomes a mania, an obsession. Their judgment becomes warped; they lose all sense of right and wrong."

"There's something else I want to ask you. What do you think of Signor Keralio?"

He hesitated a moment before he answered. Then, with some warmth, he said:

"As I told you before, I think he's a crook, only we can't prove it. I've been looking up his record. It's a bad one. The fellow has behaved himself so far in New York, but out West he is known under various names as one of the slickest rogues that ever escaped hanging. At one time he was the chief of a band of international crooks and blackmailers that operated in London, Paris, Buenos Ayres, and the City of Mexico. The scheme they usually worked was to get some prominent man so badly compromised that he would pay any amount to save himself from exposure, and they played so successfully on the fears of their victims that they were usually successful."

A worried look came into the young wife's face. Perhaps there was more in Signor Keralio's relations with her husband than she had suspected. Quickly she asked:

"Why do they permit a man of that character to be at large?"

The lawyer shrugged his shoulders.

"You can't proceed against a man unless there is some specific charge made. The police have nothing now against him. He may have reformed for all I know. But that was his record some years ago."

"I don't think he'll dare come here again," went on Helen. "He's exceedingly offensive, and yet he has about him a certain magnetism that compels your attention, even while his manner and look repels and irritates. Only the other day he—"

Before she could complete the sentence, there was a loud ring at the front door bell. Helen hastily rose, but Ray had already gone forward.

"It's Mr. Parker," she cried. "I saw him coming from the window."

The next instant the door of the drawing-room was flung open and Mr. Parker appeared.

"Hallo, ladies! Howdy, Steell!"

The president of the Americo-African Mining Company was not looking his usual debonair self that evening. His manner was nervous and flustered, his face pale and drawn with anxious lines. His coat lacked the customary boutonniere, and his crumpled linen and unshaved chin suggested that he had come direct from his office after a strenuous day without stopping to go through the formality of making a change of attire.

Helen was quick to note the alteration in his appearance, and her first instinct, naturally, was to associate it with her husband. Something was amiss.

"There's nothing wrong, is there?" she asked in alarm.

"No, no, my dear woman!"

But his tone was not convincing. He always called her "my dear woman" when nervous or excited, and "my dear lady" in his calmer moods. She at once remarked it, and it did not tend to reassure her. Now greatly alarmed she laid a trembling hand on his arm.

"Tell me, please! Don't hide anything from me. Has anything happened to Kenneth?"

"No—no; of course not." Quickly changing the subject he asked: "You got a message."

"Yes—a cablegram. It came just now."

"Have you got it? Let me see it."

"Yes, certainly," said Helen, looking around for the dispatch. Unable to find it, she called to her sister.

"Ray, dear, what did you do with Kenneth's cablegram?"

Her sister came up to assist in the search, in which even Mr. Steell joined. But the search was fruitless. The cablegram had disappeared.

"Oh, I know!" suddenly exclaimed Ray. "It must have been carried away with the tea things."

"That's right! I never thought of that!" said Helen.

The next instant the two women hurried out of the room in the direction of the kitchen.

Arthur Hornblow

The instant they had disappeared Mr. Parker turned to the lawyer. In a whisper he said:

"There is terrible news! I don't know how to break it to the poor woman—"

Steell sprang forward. Anxiously he exclaimed:

"Terrible news? Surely not—"

The president nodded.

"Yes—all lost, and the diamonds, too. A dispatch just received in London says that, according to a wireless relayed from Cape Town, the *Abyssinia* caught fire twelve hours after sailing from that port and all on board perished. It is shocking, and the pecuniary loss to us disastrous. The stones were not insured. Hush! Here they come. Not a word!"

"My God!" muttered the lawyer, as he fell back and turned away, so they might not see the effect which the shocking news had made on him. With an effort he managed to control himself.

The two women entered the room joyfully.

"Here it is!" cried Helen exultantly, as she brandished the missing telegram. "You see, he's just sailed, and all's well."

The president said nothing, but, taking the dispatch from her hands, slowly read it. Nodding his head, he said slowly:

"Yes—he's just sailed, and—all's well."

"When do you think he'll be here?" questioned the young hostess, looking anxiously up into his face.

The president shook his head.

"That is hard to tell," he answered evasively.

Mr. Steell had gone to the window, where he stood looking out, idly drumming his fingers on the pane. How was it possible to break such fearful tidings as that? What a horrible calamity! He wished himself a hundred miles away, yet some one must tell her. At that moment shrill cries arose in the street outside—the familiar, distressing, almost exultant cries of news-venders, glad of any calamity that puts a few nickels into their pockets.

"*Ex-tra! Ex-tra! Special ex-tra!*"

"What's that?" exclaimed Helen apprehensively. The sound of special editions always filled her with anxiety, especially since Kenneth's departure.

"*Ex-tra! Ex-tra! Special edition! Ex-tra! Big steamer gone down. Great loss of life. Extra!*"

Her face was pale, as she turned and looked at the others, who also stood in silence, listening to the hoarse accents of distress.

"A steamer gone down!" she faltered. "Isn't that terrible? I wonder what steamer it was."

Ray ran to the door.

"I'll get a paper," she said.

Before Mr. Parker or Mr. Steell could prevent her the young girl had opened the front door. Now there was no way of preventing Helen knowing. The best thing was to prepare her gently.

"My dear Mrs. Traynor—I didn't tell you the trouble just now. There has been a little trouble. The *Abyssinia*—"

Helen gave a cry of anguish.

Arthur Hornblow

"I knew it! I knew it! Kenneth is dead!"

"No, no, my dear lady. These newspaper reports are always grossly exaggerated. The *Abyssinia* has met with a little trouble—nothing very serious, I assure you. Everything is all right, no doubt. Your husband is well able to take care of himself. We may hear from him any moment, reassuring us as to his safety."

His words of comfort went unheeded. Her face white as death Helen tottered rather than walked to the door, reaching it just as Ray, almost as pale, entered, reading the paper she had just purchased. On seeing her sister she instinctively made an effort to hide the sheet, but Helen quickly snatched it out of her hand. Her hand trembling so violently that she could scarcely make out the letters she glanced at the big scare-head, printed in red ink, to imitate blood, a merciful custom sensational newspapers have of making the most of the agony of others.

S. S. ABYSSINIA GONE DOWN! ALL PERISH!

For a moment she stood still, looking at the big type with open, staring eyes. Then, with a low cry, like a wounded animal, she let the paper slip from her nerveless fingers. There was a furious throbbing at her temples: her heart seemed to stop. The room spun round, and she fainted just as Steell rushed forward to catch her in his arms.

"Brandy! Brandy!" he shouted. "She's fainted!"

While Ray ran for the smelling salts and Mr. Parker was bringing the brandy there came another vigorous pull at the bell. An instant later the maid entered with a cablegram, which Mr. Parker seized and tore open. As he read the contents, a look of the greatest surprise and joy lit up his face.

"Look at this!" he cried.

"What is it?" demanded Steell, still on his knees trying to

revive the unconscious woman.

"This will do her more good than all your brandy."

"What is it?" cried Ray impatiently.

"He's safe!" cried Mr. Parker exultantly.

"Safe!" they all cried.

"Yes—safe." Handing the dispatch to the lawyer, he added: "Here—read this."

Steell took the dispatch and read:

> CAPE TOWN, Saturday: Miraculously saved. Sail to-morrow on the *Zanzibar*. KENNETH.

CHAPTER XI

The house of mourning had suddenly become transformed into a house of joy.

From the deepest abyss of hopeless despair Helen, during the next few days, was raised to the highest pinnacle of human felicity. Kenneth was safe, that was all she wanted to know. Whether he had succeeded or not in saving the diamonds she did not know or care.

Nothing more had been heard from him. Cable dispatches reported the *Zanzibar* to be making good time on her way to Southampton, but, until the steamer arrived there, no further details were to be expected. Much, however, had been gleaned as to the fate of the *Abyssinia*, and, as the accounts of disaster began to come in, she could only thank God that he had succeeded in escaping such a fearful fate. The ship had mysteriously caught fire the first day out from Cape Town, and, in the excitement, the crew, as well as the passengers, lost their heads. Only one boat could be lowered, and in this Kenneth got away, together with Francois, his valet, and some other passengers. A news item in connection with the affair, which was of particular interest to Helen, ran as follows:

"The loss of the *Abyssinia* brought to a tragic ending a remarkable romance in which Mr. Kenneth Traynor, one of the rescued passengers and a prominent New York broker, is one of the principal figures. Mr. Traynor is one of two twins so identical in appearance that no one, not even their own mother, knew them apart. One of the children mysteriously disappeared when a mere child and was believed to be dead. Mr. Kenneth Traynor went recently to South Africa on business, and on the diamond fields found in starving condition an unlucky miner who was a perfect counterpart of himself. It was his lost brother. Mutual explanations followed and the identity was established. Overjoyed at the reunion the two brothers sailed for home on the *Abyssinia*. Suddenly came the alarm of fire. While the panic on board was at its worst, the broker lost sight of his brother, whom he never saw again and whom it is only too certain went down with the ship."

"It's almost unbelievable, isn't it?" exclaimed Helen, as she read the paragraph for the hundredth time and handed it to Wilbur Steell, who had dropped in to hear if there was any news.

Ray, who loved a mystery better than anything else in the world, clapped her hands.

"Isn't it perfectly stunning?"

"Not for Kenneth's brother—poor fellow," said Helen reprovingly. "He did not live long to enjoy his bettered condition."

"That's right. How thoughtless of me!" said Ray contritely.

As he finished reading Mr. Steell looked puzzled. Looking toward Helen he asked:

"Did you know that your husband had a twin brother?"

"I only knew it recently—just before he sailed. He did not know it himself."

"How did he find it out?"

"His old nurse told him. I was present."

"Did the nurse know the brother was in South Africa?"

"No—she had no idea of it. I'm sure of that. It's one of those wonderful coincidences one some-times hears of."

The lawyer shook his head. Thoughtfully he said:

"It's certainly strange—one of the strangest things I ever heard of."

"Kenneth will be able to tell us more about it when he comes," said Ray.

"Yes—no doubt," asserted her sister quickly.

The lawyer remained thoughtful for a moment. Then, lightly he said:

"We ought to give Kenneth a rousing welcome home. After such experiences as he has had he richly deserves it."

Eagerly Helen caught at the suggestion.

"By all means!" she cried. "Suppose we give a dinner, followed by a dance."

"Oh, lovely!" said Ray.

"The night following his arrival," went on Helen enthusiastically. "We'll make it quite an affair and invite everyone we know—the Parkers, the Galloways, the Fentons, everybody—"

"Don't forget me!" interrupted Steell.

"Oh, you, of course!" Roguishly she added: "Aren't you one of the family?"

He looked at her and smiled. In an undertone which Ray, too busy looking at the paper, did not hear, he added:

"Not yet, but I hope to be."

"The sooner the better, Wilbur," she said earnestly. With a significant glance at her sister she added, "Don't let her keep you waiting too long."

Every hour brought nearer the happy day when they would see Kenneth again. A cablegram from England reported that the *Zanzibar* had reached Southampton. Closely following this came a brief message from Kenneth himself, stating that he was on the point of sailing for New York on the *Adriatic*. In five more days he would be in New York.

Expectation now reached fever heat, the excitement being communicated to everyone in the house. Every time the front door bell rang there was a rush downstairs in the hope that it might be another message.

Ray, bubbling over with excitement, was almost as eager as her sister.

"Won't it be jolly to go down to the dock and meet him?"

Helen shook her head.

"I won't go to meet him. I prefer to be here when he arrives." Anxiously she added: "I hope everything is all right."

"Why shouldn't it be all right?"

Her sister was silent. It seemed absurd, when everything seemed to point to her happiness, that she should still feel depressed and nervous, but, somehow, she could not shake off the feeling that something was wrong. It was certainly strange that no letter had been received from Kenneth since the accident. Yet perhaps it was wicked of her to expect more. She ought to be grateful that he had been spared. Almost unconsciously she remarked:

"Isn't it strange that Ken hasn't written for so long? I haven't had a line from him since he left Cape Town."

"Yes—you have," protested her sister. "You had a cablegram telling you of his safety."

"A cablegram—yes, but no letter. I have had no letter since he left Cape Town."

"That's true. But how could he write? He has been traveling faster than the mails."

"I hope he's not hurt."

"Of course not. You would have heard it before this. Bad news travels fast."

Every moment from now on was devoted to getting the house ready for the arrival of its lord and master. Ray had skilfully fashioned out of red letters on white paper, a big "Welcome" sign, which was to be suspended in the hall on the complacent horns of two gigantic moose heads, souvenirs of a month's vacation in the Adirondacks. While this was being done downstairs Helen busied herself in the library and bedroom, getting ready the things for his comfort—his dressing-gown, his slippers, his pipe. She detested pipes, as do most women, but she could not refrain from giving this pipe a furtive kiss, as she laid it lovingly on the table within easy reach of the arm-chair. The maids, changed since he went away, were laboriously instructed in what they should and should not do, what towels should be put in the luxurious bathroom, what pajamas should be laid on the bed.

Well Helen remembered the first time she had entered this bedroom. Just married, in the full flush of her new-found happiness, it had all seemed so beautiful, so ideal. The dull pink color scheme, so chaste and delicate, the gracefully carved furniture, so luxurious and elegant, the cupids flying above the massive beautifully carved bed, a veritable bower of love—all this seemed only a realization of her girlhood dreams of what married life should be. And now Kenneth was coming back, after his long absence in South Africa, it would be like getting married all over again.

The next four days seemed longer than any Helen had ever spent in all her life. The delay was interminable. The minutes appeared to be like hours, the hours like days. Having to wait patiently for what one desired so ardently was simply intolerable. She tried to divert her mind by busying herself about the library, dusting his favorite books, tidying his papers, but constantly came back the thoughts that filled her with uneasiness, a vague, undefinable alarm. Was he all right?

At last the great day arrived. A Western Union telegram announced that the *Adriatic* would dock at 2 o'clock. Long before that time, Ray, unable to restrain her impatience, was on her way down town, accompanied by Mr. Steell, while Helen, her face a little paler than usual, her heart beating a little faster, sat in the great recessed window of the library, and waited for the arrival of the loved one.

Anxiously, impatiently, she watched the hands of the clock move round. How exasperatingly slow it was: how indifferent it seemed to her happiness! If the ship docked at two they could hardly arrive at the house until four. It would take at least two hours to get through the customs. Oh, would the moment never come when she would see his dear face and clasp him in her arms?

It was nearly half past two when suddenly the front door bell rang. Her heart leaping to her mouth, she rushed to the top of the stairs. It was only Mr. Parker, who had dropped in on the chance of finding his associate already arrived.

To-day the president of the Americo-African Mining Company was in the highest spirits. Everything had gone according to his expectations. Kenneth was home with the big diamonds safe in his possession. The directors could not fail to give him

(Parker) credit for his sagacity and enterprise. The stocks of the company would soar above par. Fortune was smiling on them in no uncertain way. Was it a wonder he was feeling in the best of humors?

"How do you know the diamonds are safe?" questioned Helen anxiously. "In such a terrible panic as there must have been on that ship a man thinks only of saving himself."

"Pshaw!" replied the president confidently. "I'm as sure of it as that I'm here. It was understood that he was never to part with the stones under any circumstances. They are in a belt he wears round his waist next to his skin. If the diamonds were not here, Kenneth would not be here. Knowing he is safe I am convinced that they are safe."

"Will you wait here until he comes?"

"No, I can't. There's a meeting of the directors this afternoon. I must attend. I'll call him up on the telephone—"

"But you are coming to dinner this evening—"

"Yes, yes, of course." With a smile he added: "Now, don't get too spoony when he comes, or else Ken will have no head for business."

"No fear," laughed Helen. "We are too long married for that."

"Well, good-bye. I'll see you later."

The president took his hat and turned to go. As he reached the door he turned round.

"By the bye, have you seen Signor Keralio lately?"

Helen's face grew more serious.

"No—Signor Keralio does not call here any more-at

my request."

The president gave a low, expressive whistle. Holding out his hand he said:

"Got his walking papers, eh? Well, I guess if you don't like him he isn't much good. I never did care for the look of him."

"Why did you ask?" she inquired.

"I was just curious—that's all. He's a persistent, uncomfortable kind of man. I don't like his face. It's a face I wouldn't trust—"

"That's why he's not coming here any more," she replied calmly. "He forgot himself and that was the end—"

The president turned to go.

"Well, good-bye. Ken will be here soon."

"Good-bye."

He went away, and once more Helen resumed her lonely vigil at the library window, straining her ears to catch the direction of every passing car, catching her breath with suspense as each pedestrian came into view. They could not be much longer. She wondered if he had missed her as much as she had him. No, men do not feel these things in the way women do. They are too busy—their minds too much preoccupied with their work. The turmoil of affairs absorbed their attention.

The clock struck the three-quarters, and the reverberations of the chimes had not entirely died away, when through the partly opened window came the sound of a taxicab suddenly stopping in front of the door.

At last he had come! It was surely Kenneth. Her bosom heaving with suppressed excitement she ran to the stairs and was already in the lower hall before the maid had answered the bell. Quickly she threw open the door, eager to throw herself in the traveler's arms. A tall shadow darkened the doorway. It was Francois, the French valet. Helen fell back in dismay.

"Oh, it's you!" she exclaimed, looking over his shoulder to see if Kenneth were following. "Where is your master?"

A curious expression, half-defiant, half-cunning, came over the servant's face, as he replied:

"Monsieur coming. He sent me ahead with light baggage. He detained at customs."

"Oh!" she exclaimed, disappointed. "When will he be here?"

"He come presently—perhaps quarter of an hour."

"How is your master?"

"He very well, except his eyes—they bother him a leetle."

Helen stared at him in alarm.

"His eyes," she exclaimed. "What is the matter with his eyes?"

The valet avoided her direct gaze, and, shifting uneasily on his feet, began to fuss with the leather bags he was carrying. Awkwardly he said:

"Didn't madame hear?"

"Hear what?" she gasped, now thoroughly alarmed.

The man put out his hand deprecatingly.

"Oh, it's nothing to make madame afraid. It will soon be all right. I assure madame—"

"But tell me what it is, will you?" she interrupted impatiently. "Don't have so much to say—tell me what it is—"

"It was when the ship caught fire, madame. We were running to ze life-boat, monsieur and me, when suddenly—"

"Well—what?" she almost shouted, in agony of suspense.

"Monsieur tripped over a coil of rope and fell—"

Almost unconscious in her excitement of what she was doing Helen laid her hand on the man's arm. Terror-stricken she cried:

"He didn't hurt himself seriously, did he?"

The valet shook his head.

"No, madame—not seriously. He struck his head against a chair and just graze ze eye. It is nothing serious, I assure madame. The doctor says that if he wears blue spectacles for few months he will be all right."

"Oh, he wears blue spectacles, does he?"

"Yes, madame, he must. Ze eye is inflamed and cannot stand ze strong light."

"Poor Kenneth!" she murmured, half-aloud. "I shall hardly know him in blue spectacles."

The valet, who had been watching her like a hawk out of his half-closed, sleepy-looking eyes, overheard the remark. Quickly he said:

"Of course, madame must expect to find monsieur a little changed. What we went through was *epouvantable*, something awful. We just escaped with our lives. For days monsieur was so nervous he was hardly able to speak a word. Even now he stops at times—"

Helen looked at him in wonder.

"'He stops!' What do you mean?"

The valet turned away, and for a moment was silent. Then, as if making a great effort, he turned and said:

"Madame will pardon me, but she must be brave and not show monsieur she notices any change. Ze doctor said it was a terrible shock to his nervous system—that fire. Monsieur has not been ze same since, *pas du tout* ze same. Ze doctor he says that these symptoms will all disappear once he gets home and has a good rest. It is only ze shock, I assure madame."

Helen listened appalled, her face growing whiter each moment, her lips trembling. He had met with an accident, then, after all! Her instinct had spoken truly. Her darling was ill. That explained his long silence. He had been too ill to write. He had gone through a terrible shock and he had come home ill, very ill, quite changed. Her voice faltering she said:

"What are the symptoms?"

"Monsieur's memory is so bad, madame. He forgets. Only to-day, as ze ship came up ze harbor, I ask monsieur if he expect madame to meet us at ze dock. *C'est vraiment incroyable*! He turned to me, with a look of ze greatest surprise, and asked: 'Who ze devil is madame?'"

"What! Didn't he seem to remember me, even?" A look of distress came over her face.

The valet shook his head.

"Non, madame." Quickly he added: "But it is nothing. It is only temporary."

"Didn't he know my sister and Mr. Steell? Didn't they greet him at the dock?"

"Yes, madame. They spoke to him and he spoke to them. But he was not himself. They seemed surprised. They will tell madame."

Helen fell back, sick and faint. Why had she not known this before? She would have gone down to meet him, thrown herself weeping into his arms. He would have known her then—who better than he would recognize that perfume he loved so well? He would have taken her in his strong arms and kissed her passionately. If he was not himself it was because he was ill. The shock had affected his memory! Poor darling husband, he must be well nursed. A few days of her devoted care and he would be all right again. Of course, it was nothing serious. Kenneth had led too clean and wholesome a life for anything grave to be the matter. If only he would come! God grant that he return to her as he went away!

As the unspoken prayer died away on her lips, there was the chugging of an automobile stopping suddenly at the curb.

"*Les voici!*" cried Francois, dropping into his native tongue in his excitement.

He threw open the wide doors and the next instant Ray ran up the steps. Helen, weak and dizzy from nervous tension, feeling as if she were about to faint, met her on the threshold.

"Kenneth!" she gasped. "Is he all right?"

"Certainly—he's fine. He's a little tired and nervous after the long journey, and the blue spectacles he wears make him look different, but he's all right."

The wife looked searchingly, eagerly at the young girl's face, as if seeking to read there what she dreaded to ask, and it seemed to her that the customary ring of sincerity was lacking in her sister's voice.

"Where is he—why isn't he with you?'

"Here he is now—don't you see him?"

Helen looked out. There came the tall, familiar figure she knew so well, the square shoulders, the thick bushy hair, with its single white lock so strangely isolated among the brown. Her heart fell as she saw the blue glasses. They veiled from her view those dear blue eyes, so kind and true. They made him look different. But what did she care as long as he had come home to her? Even with the horrid glasses, that dear form she would know in a thousand!

Slowly he came up the long flight of stone steps, weighted down by traveling rugs and handbag, both of which he refused to surrender to the obsequious Francois. Eagerly she rushed down the steps to meet him, her eyes half-closed, ready to swoon from excitement and joy. Nothing was said. He opened his arms. She put up her mouth, tenderly, submissively. For a moment he seemed to hesitate. He held her tight in his embrace, and just looked down at her. Then, as he felt the warmth of her soft, yielding body next to his, and saw the partly opened mouth, ready to receive his kiss, he bent down and fastened his lips on hers.

CHAPTER XII

For one blissful, ecstatic moment Helen lay tight in his embrace, nestling against the breast of the one being she loved better than anyone else in the world, responding with involuntary vibrations of her own body to the gust of fiery passion that swept his. But only for a moment. The next instant she had torn herself violently free, and was gazing, wonderingly, fearfully, up into his face, trying to penetrate those glasses which veiled, as it were, the windows of his soul. Why she broke away so abruptly from his embrace she could not herself have explained. Something within her, some instinct to which her reason was unable to give a name, made her body revolt against the unusual ardor of the caress. Strange! Never before had she felt so embarrassed at Kenneth's demonstrations of affection.

"How are you, dear?" she murmured, when at last she could find words.

She had not yet heard the sound of his beloved voice, and when at last he answered her it seemed to her ears only like an echo of its former self, so exhausted and wearied was he by what he had gone through.

"Very tired, sweetheart," he replied huskily. "I shall need a long rest."

She led the way into the house and up the stairs, where everything had been so elaborately prepared for his welcome.

In the bedroom she pointed with pride to the real Valenciennes lace coverlet put on in his honor, and showed him the dressing-gown and slippers so lovingly laid out. He looked at everything, but made no comment. She half expected a few words of praise, but none were forthcoming. While affectionately demonstrative he was unusually reticent. She wondered what worry he could have on his mind to make him act so strangely and suddenly Keralio's words of warning came to her mind. Was there a side to his life of which she knew nothing? Were his thoughts elsewhere, even while he was with her? Quickly there came a look of dismay and anxiety, which he was not slow to notice. Instantly on his guard, he murmured in a low tone:

"Forgive me, dear, I can't talk now. I'm so tired I can hardly keep my eyes open."

Instantly her apprehension was forgotten in her desire to make him comfortable.

"That's right, dear. You must be dead with fatigue. You'll take a nice nap and when you wake up it will be time for dinner. I've planned a nice little party to celebrate your return—only a few intimates—Mr. Parker is coming, and Wilbur Steell, and a young man named Dick Reynolds, an acquaintance of Wilbur's. You won't mind such old friends, will you?"

He shook his head.

"No, indeed. I'm very tired, now, but I'll be all right in a few minutes."

"Of course you will," she smiled, as she removed the handsome lace coverlet from the bed. "No one will disturb you. My darling hubbie can sleep as sound as a top, and, when he wakes, we'll talk a terrible lot, won't we?" Looking up roguishly, as she smoothed his pillow for him, she added shyly: "There are two pillows here now. There has been only one while you were away—"

For the first time he seemed to evince interest in what she was saying. His eyes flashed behind the blue spectacles, and his hands trembled, as he quickly made a step forward and put his arm round her waist.

"There'll always be two in the future, won't there?" he asked hoarsely.

"Yes, of course there will," she laughed,

"To-night?" he insisted.

"Yes, of course," she said, her color heightening slightly under the persistency of his gaze. What a foolish question! Changing the topic she added, with a laugh: "Now, take your coat off, like a good boy, and go to sleep. I'll go down and keep the house quiet. When it's time to get up, I'll come back."

"Don't go yet," he murmured, looking at her ardently. Taking her hand caressingly he tried to lead her to the sofa. "Sit down here. I won't sleep yet. Let us talk. I have so much to say."

Firmly Helen withdrew from his embrace.

"No, no; I won't stay a moment," she said decisively. "Not now. You must behave yourself. We'll talk all you want to to-night. But not now. You are very tired. The sleep will do you good. Now be a good boy—go to bed."

He tried to intercept her before she reached the door, but she was too quick for him. She went out and was about to close the door behind her when he called out:

"Please send Francois to me."

She nodded.

"Yes, dear, I will. Of course you need him. Why didn't I think of it before?"

She closed the door and went downstairs. It was hard to believe that he was back home. How long she had waited for this day, and, even now it had come, the void did not seem filled. There still seemed something wanting. What it was, she did not know, yet it was there.

In the dining-room she ran into Ray, who had her arms filled with magnificent American beauty roses.

"Oh, how beautiful!" cried Helen enthusiastically. "Where did you get those flowers?"

The young girl laughed. "They're a present from me and Wilbur—in honor of Kenneth's arrival. Where is he?"

"Upstairs—he's going to lie down until dinner is ready. Poor soul—he's almost dead with fatigue."

"Has he got the diamonds?"

Helen gasped. She hadn't thought of that. In all the excitement the real object of her husband's trip to South Africa had quite escaped her mind.

"I don't know," she said quickly. "I haven't asked him. We've hardly exchanged a dozen words. He'll tell us later. Was nothing said about them at the Customs? Didn't he declare them?"

"No—I thought it was strange. That's why I asked you if he had them. Possibly he left them to be cut in Amsterdam."

Helen grew thoughtful.

"I don't know. He'll tell us later."

Ray filled the vases with the flowers, while Helen busied herself at the buffet, getting out all the pretty silverware with which the dinner table was to be decorated. The young girl hummed lightly as she decorated the room with the fragrant blossoms.

"Isn't it lovely that Kenneth is back?" she exclaimed.

"Yes, indeed."

"I hardly knew him at first in those spectacles."

"I'm not surprised at that."

"If it hadn't been for that white patch of hair I don't think we could have picked him out of the crowd. There was an awful crush there."

There was a pause, and then Helen asked:

"How do you think he looks?"

"About the same," replied the girl carelessly. "He doesn't seem in as good spirits as when he went away. He is very quiet. He hardly spoke a word to us on the way home. Possibly he has some business anxiety on his mind."

"Did he ask about me?"

"Yes—you were his first question."

"Did you tell him about Dorothy?"

"That she was not so well? Yes."

"What did he say? Was he worried?"

"Not particularly. I think men are more sensible in those matters than we women. He knows baby is well taken care of." Changing the subject, the young girl went on: "I hope everybody will be jolly to-night. I've made up my mind to have a good time."

Helen sighed.

"I'm feeling a little uneasy about Dorothy. I got a letter this morning from Aunt Carrie, saying she was not feeling so well. The doctor was going to see her to-day, and, if she got worse, they said they'd telegraph."

Ray looked at her sister in consternation.

"What would you do then?"

"I would have to go at once to Philadelphia."

"And Kenneth just come home—oh, Helen!"

"I couldn't help it. Kenneth couldn't go. Somebody must go. The child could not be left alone. Who should go better than its mother?"

Ray made a gesture of protest.

"Well, don't let's imagine the worst. Dorothy won't get worse. To-morrow you'll get a reassuring letter, and your worries will be over."

"I hope so," smiled Helen.

Leaving the task of sorting the knives and forks Ray came over to where Helen was standing. The young girl pointed to all the vases filled with the crimson roses.

"How do you like that?" she exclaimed.

"Beautiful!"

There was a brief silence, both women being preoccupied by their thoughts, when Ray, in her usual vivacious, impulsive way, burst out:

"Sis, I have something to tell you."

Helen looked up quickly.

"Something to tell me—something good?"

"I'm so happy! I'm engaged at last."

"To Wilbur, of course?"

"Yes."

Helen gave an exclamation of joy.

"Oh, I'm so glad. When did it happen? Tell me all about it— quick."

"He proposed to-day, and I said yes. We're to be married in two months."

The next moment the two women were in each other's arms.

"I'm so glad—so glad," murmured Helen. "I hope you'll both be very, very happy."

"We certainly shall if we are like you and Kenneth. Wilbur says that your example is the one thing that decided him to make the plunge."

Helen smiled.

"You'll have one advantage I don't enjoy. Your husband, being a lawyer, won't be taking trips to South Africa all the time."

"Oh, I don't know," laughed the girl; "it's sometimes nice to lose sight of each other for a time. The lovemaking is all the more furious when your husband gets back."

"Yes—unless he happens to meet some other charmer on

his travels."

"Oh, nonsense, Helen—men don't really have such adventures. That only happens in novels."

"I hope so," murmured her sister.

"Oh, by the bye," exclaimed Ray, "who do you suppose we saw on the dock?"

"Who?"

"That horrid creature—Signor Keralio."

Helen looked up in surprise.

"Keralio? What was he doing there? Did he speak to you?"

"No—he seemed to avoid us. Once I got lost for a moment in the crush, and, as I turned, I thought I saw him talking earnestly to Kenneth and Francois. Of course I must have been mistaken, for, when I finally rejoined them, both denied having seen him!"

"Keralio!" murmured Helen. "How strange! That man seems to pursue us like some evil genius. No matter where we go, he follows like a shadow. Oh, I forgot all about Francois. Where is he?"

"Downstairs."

Helen touched a bell.

"Why do you need him?"

"Kenneth wants him. I forgot all about it. All his things need putting away. The litter upstairs is simply terrible."

"There won't be much time for unpacking," objected Ray.

"It's half-past five already. We'll soon have to think of dressing for dinner."

Suddenly the door opened and Francois appeared. He entered quietly, stealthily, and, advancing to where his mistress was, stood in silence, awaiting her orders.

"Your master wants you upstairs, Francois."

The man bowed.

"*Bien*, madame!"

"Tell Mr. Traynor not to keep you too long, because there's a lot of work to be done downstairs before dinner."

"*Bien*, madame."

The man lingered in the room, arranging the chairs, and fussing about the table, until he began to make Helen nervous. Peremptorily she said:

"You had better go, Francois; monsieur is waiting for you."

The valet bowed obsequiously, and left the room, shutting the door carefully. Instead of proceeding immediately upstairs, he stopped for a moment behind the closed door and listened intently. But, unable to overhear the two women, who were conversing in an undertone, he hurried upstairs toward his employer's bedroom. Arrived on the landing, he went straight to the room, and, without stopping for the formality of knocking, he turned the handle and went in.

CHAPTER XIII

Instead of finding his master resting from his fatigue, as Mrs. Traynor had said, Francois discovered the new arrival very much awake. He was sitting in front of Helen's bureau, eagerly perusing a bundle of private letters tied with blue ribbon, which he had taken from a drawer. As the door opened, he jumped up quickly, as if detected committing a dishonorable action; but, when he saw who it was, his face relaxed and he gave a grim nod of recognition.

"Lock the door!" he said in a whisper. "It won't do to have anyone come in here now."

The valet turned the key, and, dropping entirely the obsequious manner of the paid menial, threw himself carelessly into a chair. Taking from his pocket a richly chased silver cigarette box, loot from former houses where he had been employed, he struck a match on the highly polished Circassian walnut chair, and proceeded to enjoy a smoke.

His companion looked at him anxiously.

"Well?" he demanded hoarsely. "Is it all right? What do they say? Does anyone suspect?"

The Frenchman gracefully emitted from between his thin lips a thick cloud of blue smoke, and broke into a laugh that, under the circumstances, sounded strangely hollow and sinister.

"Suspect?" he chuckled. "Why should they suspect? Are you not ze same man who went away—ze same build, ze same face, ze same voice, ze same in every particular—except one. Zat you have not—*non*—you have not ze education, ze fine manners, ze *savoir faire* of monsieur." With that expressive shrug of the shoulder, so characteristic of his nation, he added: "*Mais que voulez vous?* We must do ze best we can."

His listener struck the brass bed-post savagely with his heavy fist. With a burst of profanity he broke out:

"Yes, damn him! He had all the advantages. I had none. But it's my turn now. I want all that's coming to me."

"Hush!" exclaimed the valet, raising his finger warningly. "Zey may hear. Everything will be all right. We must be very careful. You must not talk. You must avoid people. Let them think you sick, or strange, or crazy, anything you like. But keep away from zem, or else they soon discover that 'Handsome Jack,' ze penniless adventurer, is quite a different person from ze accomplished and wealthy Monsieur Kenneth Traynor."

"We can't expect to keep the game up long," interrupted the big fellow moodily.

"We won't have to," replied his companion calmly. "Just enough time to squeeze ze orange dry—that's all—"

Handsome looked up quickly. Savagely he retorted:

"Of which juice you and Keralio want a goodly share, don't you?"

The valet's greenish eyes flashed.

"Of course I do, and, what's more, I mean to get it." Changing his free, careless tone to one tense with significance and menace he went on: "Don't be a fool, Monsieur Handsome.

Who put you up to this snap, but me? Who knows what you did to monsieur out there on ze *veldt*, better than me? Dead men tell no tales, but live ones do. Don't forget that! If you want to keep clear of ze electric chair, you'll keep your mouth shut, and play fair."

The gambler listened, his mouth twitching nervously, his eyes glowing with sullen hatred.

"What do you and Keralio want? I gave you the diamonds—what more do you expect?"

The valet laughed scoffingly.

"You gave him ze diamonds. Why? You were d—d glad to be rid of zem. We can't do anything with zem now. We may have to wait months or years before we can venture to cut zem up and dispose of zem. *Non*, monsieur! If zey appeared on ze market now, ze news would be flashed *immediatement* to every corner of ze globe, and your career and mine would come to a quick end. *Voila!*"

"Don't forget Keralio!" said Handsome, with a sneer.

"*Eh, bien*? Has he not earned it, Signor Keralio? Is it not because of his courage and daring that you are here—ze master in this house? Who but Keralio would have had ze nerve to carry ze thing through?"

Handsome shrugged his shoulders. Cynically he said:

"Oh, I don't know. It seems to me that Keralio is safe under cover, while here I am, disporting myself in the limelight, with every eye turned on me. I guess I prefer Keralio's job to mine—"

The valet's eyes flashed vindictively as he retorted:

"Could your puny brain have conceived this scheme which will make us all rich? Keralio outlined ze whole plan to me directly he heard of your existence. On our reaching Cape Town, after finding you starving on ze *veldt*, I cabled him ze news. A few hours later he told me exactly what to do. He knew you would do it. How, I do not know. He is no ordinary man, Keralio. When I first saw you out zere, unkempt, in rags, starving, I could have dropped dead from surprise. It never occurred to me that you might be useful. But Keralio knew. He knows everything. He also knew that you would accept his leadership, that you would quickly get rid of monsieur, and secure ze diamonds. Was it not his idea that you set fire to ze ship? And who set fire to ze ship, *s'il vous plait*, when you refused? Who but your very humble servant. And a hard, dangerous job, it was, too—catch me ever wanting to do it again!"

"Not half so bad as mine. He put up a terrible fight before I threw him overboard."

"Who—monsieur?"

"Yes—he fought like a wildcat, and he was fast getting the best of me, when I managed to give him a rap on the head. That quieted him, and over he went." With an exclamation of disgust, he added: "It was a d—d nasty job. I'm sorry I ever went into it—"

"Sorry—you fool? *Sapristi*! Just think of this wonderful opportunity. You have ze keys to his vaults, you have control of his bank accounts." Lowering his voice, and, with a significant leer on his face, he added "and you have—his wife!"

Handsome grinned, and the valet went on:

"*Precisement*! Madame is cold and haughty, like all zese American women. It's not exactly my taste, but she's pretty and dainty, and—"

"Who are all these other people," interrupted the miner, "that man Steell—"

"Yes, that is so. You must know everyone. You must make a study of each, so as to avoid making bad breaks. Monsieur Steell is a lawyer. He's in love with madame's sister, Miss Ray. You've known him all your life, went to school with him, and all that sort of thing. Say 'yes' to everything he says. That's your cue at present. Talk as little as you can, and agree with everybody. The man you must talk with most is Monsieur Parker. He is president of the mining company. Happily he's rather shortsighted, so he won't notice anything. He's the man to whom you'll have to explain ze loss of ze diamonds. He'll be here to-night for dinner, so you'd better get your story ready."

"What can I say?"

"Say that in ze panic your belt worked loose, you had to dive into ze water. When you were dragged into ze lifeboat the belt was gone, do you understand?"

"Yes—but will they believe it?"

"They must believe it. There'll be an awful fuss, of course, but they'll get over it. No suspicion can attach to you."

"He's coming to-night—this man Parker?"

"Yes, to-night. He'll be here for dinner. He—"

Before the valet could complete the sentence there was a knock on the door and Helen outside called out:

"May I come in?"

Instantly the valet jumped up and assumed once more his deferential demeanor. The gambler hurriedly shut the bureau drawers and put on the blue spectacles.

The door opened and Helen entered.

Alert as the Frenchman was, he was not quick enough to quite conceal from the wife that his present obsequious manner had been suddenly assumed for her benefit directly she had entered the room. She had overheard voices, as she reached the landing, and the abrupt manner in which these sounds had ceased was not entirely natural. It had also seemed to her that the valet's tone had had a ring of familiarity about it which she had never known it to have before. Could it be possible that they were discussing matters which were to be kept from her? If so, her husband already had secrets in which not she but his valet shared. She recalled Keralio's cynical smile, as he had whispered: "Husbands only tell their wives half." Perhaps he had spoken the truth. Perhaps at this very moment she was degraded, insulted in her womanhood by a man who was secretly unloyal to her. The very thought went through her like a knife-thrust. All her life, every hour she had devoted to her husband. Even now she did not like to even harbor a shade of distrust, but his strange behavior since his return, this earnest conversation behind closed doors with a menial she despised and distrusted—all this could not but add to her anxiety. Calmly, she asked:

"Have you finished with Francois, dear? We need him downstairs."

The valet himself answered the question:

"*Oui*, madame. I was just coming."

Bowing politely, he turned on his heel, and, with a significant glance at Handsome, which his mistress did not notice, he left the room. Helen glanced at the bed, which was undisturbed. Surprised, she exclaimed:

"Why, I thought you were going to lie down!"

He shook his head. Shifting uneasily on his feet, and, without looking up, he answered:

"No—I can't sleep. I'm too nervous. I'll sleep to-night."

Advancing farther into the room she went up him and put her arm affectionately round him. Sympathetically she said:

"You'll feel better in a few days, dear. Just rest and take things easy. I won't hear of your going to the office for a week at least. All the business you and Mr. Parker have you can transact here. By the way, dear, you haven't even mentioned the most important thing of all—have you brought back the diamonds?"

Instead of replying at once to her question, he turned quickly and pulled down the blind.

"You don't mind, do you?" he said. "The light hurts my eyes."

"Of course not," she replied. Sitting down near him she went on: "Tell me—have you got the diamonds? How beautiful they must be! How I should love to see them!"

When finally he turned and confronted her she could see his face only indistinctly, as the drawing of the blind had left the room almost in darkness. His voice was strained and tense as he replied huskily:

"I have not got the diamonds!"

Helen almost started from her seat.

"You have not got them!" she exclaimed. "Where are they, Ken?"

"They are lost!"

"Lost?" she echoed, stupefied.

"Yes—lost."

"Oh, how terrible!" she faltered.

This, then, was the secret of his strange manner, his depression and nervousness. He had lost the diamonds. He had returned home to announce to the eagerly awaiting stockholders that over a million dollars' worth of property had suddenly been swept away. His feeling of personal responsibility must have been awful. No wonder he was not himself. It was enough to unnerve any man. Of course he was not to blame, but the world is so merciless. He would have to bear the censure, even when he was perfectly innocent. How she regretted that he had ever undertaken so heavy a responsibility. Timidly, not wishing to embarrass or annoy him, she said:

"How did it happen, dear?"

For a moment he made no answer, but just sat and stared at her. What little light entered between the shade and the window frame fell full on her face, lighting up the fine profile, the delicately chiseled mouth, throwing off golden glints from her artistically arranged hair. From her face his eyes wandered greedily down to her snow-white neck, her slender, graceful figure, her beautifully molded arms. Certainly, he mused to himself, his brother was an epicure in love. This woman was dainty enough to tempt a saint.

"How did it happen?" she asked again.

"It was in the first rush from the burning ship," he said hoarsely. "I was asleep when the fire broke out. It happened at two o'clock in the morning. The diamonds were in the belt which each night I unfastened and put under my pillow. It was more comfortable to do that than to wear it. When the first alarm came I forgot everything—except my own safety. I rushed pell-mell on deck. It was a nasty night. We didn't know where we were, or how grave the situation was. Outside the wind was howling furiously, the siren was blowing dismally, the panic-stricken passengers and sailors were fighting like wildcats. I lost my head along with the rest. I had reached the lifeboat when suddenly I remembered the belt. I felt at my waist. It was not there. I remembered I had left it under the pillow. I was horror-stricken. Great beads of perspiration broke from every pore. The people were fighting to get into the boat; I fought to get out and back to my stateroom. Suddenly someone knocked me on the head. I lost consciousness. When I came to we were miles away from the wreck, drifting on the ocean in an open boat, and the *Abyssinia* was nowhere to be seen."

Helen made an exclamation of sympathy.

"Poor soul—how terrible you must have felt! Thank God, you escaped with your life! We ought to feel grateful for that. Suppose I had been compelled to tell Mary that you were drowned. It would have killed her—you know that. Do you remember what you told her when you went away?"

He stared at her, not understanding.

"Told who?" he said cautiously.

"Mary."

"Oh, yes—Mary—of course—you mean your sister—"

Helen looked at him in amazement, then in alarm. Could the wreck have affected his mind? Laughingly she retorted:

"Ray? Of course not. How foolish you are, Kenneth. Don't you remember that your old nurse came to see you before you sailed?"

He nodded and coughed uneasily, moving restlessly about in his chair, as if to hide his embarrassment. These questions were decidedly unpleasant. Inwardly he wished Francois was present to help him out.

"Mary? Oh, yes, I remember—of course—of course—"

The look of anxiety in the young woman's face deepened. His

memory failed him completely. Changing the subject she said quickly:

"There's something else I wish to mention to you, dear. It is about Signor Keralio—"

He started quickly to his feet. How came his brother's wife to know the name of the arch-plotter, the man who had sentenced her own husband to death? Was it possible that she knew more? Was she aware of his real identity? Was her present amiability of manner merely simulated? Was she waiting her time before calling in the police and exposing him as an impostor?

"Keralio?" he echoed hoarsely. "What about Keralio?" Making a step forward he exclaimed savagely: "Has he squealed? Is the game up? He's to blame, not I!"

Impulsively, instinctively, Helen sprang from her chair and fell back with a startled exclamation. Now thoroughly alarmed, more than ever convinced that the shipwreck had affected his brain, her one solicitude was to keep him quiet until she could get a doctor. Soothingly she said:

"Of course, dear; of course. We won't speak of Signor Keralio now. He's not worth discussing anyhow."

He watched her closely for a moment, as if trying to see if she were deceiving him, but her face was frank and serene. Suddenly, taking hold of her hand, which she abandoned willingly enough in his, he murmured:

"You mustn't mind what I say. I'll soon be all right. I'm a bit mixed up. My mind's been queer ever since that awful night."

"Perhaps you would prefer if we had no one to dinner. I could easily give some excuse and put them all off."

His first impulse was to promptly accept this suggestion, yet

what was the good? If he did not meet them to-day he must do
so to-morrow. It was best to get it over with. The quicker he
got to know the people the easier it would be for him. If he
seemed to avoid meeting them, it might only arouse suspicion.
Shaking his head, he said:

"No, dear. That's all right. I'm glad they're coming. It will
liven things up."

Helen's face brightened. It was the first cheerful remark he had
made.

"That's what I think. You must forget what you have gone
through. After all it's not so bad, but it might be a lot worse.
Mr. Parker will feel badly about the stones, of course, because
he had counted on making capital out of the advertising they
would receive. But who knows? Perhaps it's all for the best.
They may find other stones even more valuable."

A sudden knock at the door interrupted them.

"Come in," called out Helen.

The maid appeared.

"Mr. Parker is downstairs, m'm."

"Good gracious! Here already for dinner. What time is it?"

"Seven o'clock, m'm."

"All right. I'll be down immediately."

The girl went away and Helen turned to her companion.

"Now, hurry, dear, won't you? Dinner is ready. The guests are
arriving. Dress quickly and come down."

He still held her hand.

"You're not angry with me?" he whispered.

"Why should I be angry?"

"Because of the diamonds."

"No, indeed—it was you I wanted, not the diamonds."

Drawing her to him, he kissed her. But her lips were cold. There was no response to his ardor. She could not herself have explained why. She felt no inclination to respond to his caresses, which at any other time she would have returned with warmth. With a slight shade of impatience she broke away.

"We have no time for that now, Kenneth. Our guests are waiting."

"That's right," he replied, with a smile that did not escape her. "We've no time now. But the night is still before us."

"Will you come soon?"

"Yes—I'll be right down."

CHAPTER XIV

Once more the Traynor residence was filled with the sounds of mirth and revelry.

From cellar to attic the old mansion was ablaze with light. The large dining-room, decorated with flowers and plants, wore a festive air, and the long table in the center literally groaned under its burden of fine linen, crystal, and silver.

The dinner, now drawing to a close, had been a huge success in every way, and, with the serving of the *demi-tasse*, the guests sat back in their chairs, feeling that sense of gluttony satisfied which only a perfect dinner can impart. The rarest wines, the richest foods—Helen had spared no expense to make the affair worthy the occasion.

As Mr. Parker sat back and with deliberation lit the big black Corona, which his host had given him, he felt as much at ease as can a man who has dined well and knows that his affairs are prospering beyond all expectations, and, as his eyes half closed, he listened dreamily while his host, for the hundredth time, told yarns of the diamond fields, he silently congratulated himself on his astuteness in having employed so successful a messenger. He had not yet had an opportunity to ask any questions about the diamonds. He had his own reasons for not wanting those present to learn too much of his plans. There would be plenty of time when he could get the vice-president alone. So he just sat back and puffed his cigar, while around him went on the hum of conversation, punctuated here and there with bursts of laughter.

Considering his short stay at the diamond mines it was astonishing how well stocked their host was with stories. To hear him talk one might have thought he had been a miner all his life. Stimulated by copious draughts of champagne, which he contrived to make flow like water, he was highly interesting, and his listeners, greatly interested, hung on to every word.

"It must be a terrible life!" said Steell, as he lit another cigar.

The host emptied his glass and again refilled it before he answered:

"It's a life of a dog—not of a human being. The toil is incessant, the profit doubtful. You starve to death: good food is unprocurable save at prohibitive prices. One sleeps practically in the open, save for such rude shelter as each man can make for himself. The flies are a pest and constant source of danger. The water is abominable."

"You like champagne better, eh?" laughed Ray.

The gambler had already drunk more than was good for him, and, raising his glass in a mock toast, began to hum the first lines of a familiar camp ditty:

> *"La femme qui sait me plaire*
> *C'est la petite veuve Clicquot."*

"Is there much stealing of diamonds by the miners?" demanded Mr. Parker.

Handsome nodded.

"Lots of it. They have to watch 'em all the time. They resort to all kinds of tricks to conceal stones they find. They used to swallow them, but when they were forced to take powerful emetics and other drugs, they soon got tired of that game.

They also try to smuggle them across the border line. One detective, who had been for months on the trail of a well-to-do smuggler, was badly stung. The man invited him to go shooting, and kindly furnished guns and cartridges. The unsuspecting policeman carried the cartridges across the border, never dreaming that each one was filled with diamonds."

Ray clapped her hands.

"Oh, what a clever idea!"

The host nodded approvingly.

"That's what I thought. Any man as smart as that deserved to get away with it."

Mr. Parker protested.

"Rogues are always smart!" he exclaimed.

"Until they're caught," laughed Dick Reynolds. "Then they don't think they're so smart."

Mr. Steell nodded approval.

"I know something about that," said the lawyer. "A crook is never really clever. He always leaves some loophole which leads to detection. He thinks he is secure, that his disguise is impenetrable, but there is always someone watching him, closely observing his every move. And, the first thing he knows, he has walked into a trap, the handcuffs are snapped, and the electric chair looms grimly before him—"

Crash!

All looked up to the end of the table, where their host had broken a glass. In the act of raising the champagne to his lips the glass had slipped and broken into a thousand pieces. Helen, frightened, started from her seat.

"Are you hurt, dear?" she asked. "There is blood on your hand."

"No—no, it's nothing. I cut myself with a bit of glass. It's nothing."

Ray was eager for more anecdotes.

"Do tell us more, Kenneth," she exclaimed, interrupting her chat with her left-hand neighbor.

"Give him a breathing spell," laughed Dick. "We've kept him at it ever since the dinner began."

Handsome, his face pale, his hand trembling, filled another glass with the foaming golden wine, and drained it at a draught. What the lawyer just said had been somewhat of a shock. Was there more meaning in it than appeared in the chance words? He eyed Steell narrowly, when he was not looking, but the lawyer's face was inscrutable. Again he filled his glass and again emptied it.

That her husband had been drinking heavily all evening had not escaped Helen's attention, and it worried her. Nudging her sister she whispered:

"Ken's drinking more than is good for him. He never used to drink like that."

At that moment, the host looked up and caught Helen's eye. Raising his glass he offered a toast:

"Here's to the prettiest, the sweetest, the most desirable little woman in the world! Gentlemen and ladies—my wife!"

They all drank except Helen who, confused and annoyed, tried to turn it off with a laugh.

Noticing her embarrassment, Ray made a signal to Mr. Steell

and they both rose from the table. Helen and Dick quickly followed their example and the hostess led the way into the drawing-room, leaving Handsome and Mr. Parker alone to their cigars.

The president of the Americo-African Mining Company was not sorry of the opportunity which this tete-a-tete afforded for a quiet business talk.

"By the way, old man," he began, "we haven't had a chance to talk business yet. You've got the diamonds, of course."

His host was silent. Mr. Parker thought he had not heard. A little louder he repeated:

"You've got the diamonds?"

Still no answer. The president began to get uneasy. Could anything be wrong or was his friend drunk? He had noticed that he had been drinking heavily—something he had never known Kenneth Traynor do. With some impatience he said sharply: "What's the matter, Kenneth? Wake up, old man. I asked you a question. Can't you answer?"

Handsome brought his fist down on the table with a bang that made the glasses dance.

"D—it!" he exclaimed angrily. "Can't a man be left alone in his own house for a few minutes without bothering him with business?"

This outburst was so utterly unexpected that Mr. Parker, taken entirely by surprise, fell back in his chair and stared at his host in amazement. Never before had he known his old friend and partner to act in this strange way. Could anything be amiss? Now he came to think of it, he had noticed a great change in his associate directly he saw him. He had seemed to lack his customary cordiality and frankness. He appeared moody and morose, as if he had on his mind some weighty responsibility he was unwilling to share. Evidently there was nothing to be gained by displaying impatience, so, in more conciliatory tones, he asked:

"That's all right, my boy. If you don't care to talk shop to-night, we won't. I didn't want to hurry you. I was curious, that's all. I have scarcely been able to curb my impatience. You understand what it means to us. Why, the very announcement that we have the diamonds safe here in New York, will be enough to send the company's stock up twenty points." Lowering his voice and bending over he added confidentially: "I don't mind telling you that I've been buying for my own account all the cheap stock I could put my hands on. As to the stockholders, they're simply wild with impatience to see the big stones. But we won't talk any more about it to-night. We'll wait till to-morrow."

Handsome, his face almost livid, leaned over the table. Hoarsely, he replied:

"It's no use waiting till to-morrow. All that's to be told can be told now. I haven't got the diamonds!"

For a moment Mr. Parker did not realize what the other man was saying. Thinking he had not heard right he asked:

"What did you say?"

"I have not got the diamonds!"

The president started from his seat. His face pale as death, his hand shaking as stricken with palsy, he almost shouted:

"You have not got the diamonds! Then where in God's name are they?"

"At the bottom of the ocean!"

The senior partner dropped back in his chair, white as death.

Then this was the outcome of all his hopes, all his planning. Faintly he gasped:

"Why didn't you tell me so before?"

"I had no opportunity. I didn't want to cable such news. It might have caused a slump in the shares. I could not let you know before. This is the first time I've seen you alone."

The president said no more. The lines about his mouth tightened and the expression of his face underwent a change. He uttered not a word, but just sat there, his eyes fixed steadily on his companion, who continued to fill his glass with champagne. Cornelius Winthrop Parker was not a man to be easily deceived. He had too much experience of the world for that. All his life he had been reading men and what he heard now in the tone of his host's voice convinced him that he was lying. That, in itself, was sufficient of a shock. To find Kenneth Traynor—the soul of integrity and honor—deliberately betraying a trust of such importance hurt him almost as much as the loss of the gems. That they had gone down with the *Abyssinia* he did not for a moment believe. It was more likely that they had been sold—possibly to make good Wall Street losses. Talk of big stock deals in which Traynor had been mixed up had reached his ear before today, and more recently this gossip had become more insistent. Kenneth was interested, said rumor, in pool operations involving millions. The recent sudden slump had found him unprepared. Ruin threatened him and to save himself he had succumbed to temptation. This, at least, was the theory which the President's alert brain rapidly evolved as he sat watching the man in front of him. Perhaps all was not yet lost. If the stones had not yet been disposed of, an effort might still be made to recover them and at the same time save Traynor and his young wife from the disgrace that such a grave scandal would entail. The first thing necessary was to keep cool, show no concern and disarm suspicion by pretending to accept the loss as irreparable. Then, at the first opportunity, he would take Wilbur Steell into his confidence. That wide awake lawyer would know exactly how to handle the case. Dick

Reynolds would have an opportunity to show his talent as a detective. Breaking the long silence he said calmly:

"Of course, I understand your silence. I think you acted wisely. We had better keep the loss to ourselves as long as we can. No one can attach any blame to you. It is a terrible loss, but we must face it like men."

The gambler looked up quickly, and eyed his guest narrowly. Seeing nothing on the latter's face to arouse his suspicions, he grew more cheerful. Less sullen and defiant, he extended his hand.

"Thanks, old man!" he exclaimed heartily. "I expected no less from you. I can't tell you how badly I feel about the loss. No doubt my manner has seemed strange since my return. I have been irritable with everybody—even my dear wife has noticed it. It was only because I did not know how to make a clear breast of it. Since you take it so sensibly, I'll cheer up. I declare I feel like a new man already."

Mr. Parker lit another cigar. Calmly, he said:

"That's right, Kenneth my boy. Keep a stiff upper lip. All's for the best. We'll have better luck next time."

As he spoke, Wilbur Steell passed on his way to join the ladies in the drawing-room. The president called out to him:

"Hello, Steell. What are you so busy about? Entertaining the women, eh? Always thought you were a lady killer. Suppose you come and smoke a cigar with me and let our friend here go and have a chat with his wife. You've no right to monopolize the fair sex in that fashion, even if you are a trust lawyer. Anyhow, I want to talk to you—just a little matter of business—that's all!"

Steell laughed, and, dropping into a chair, took the cigar which Mr. Parker held out. Turning to his host, and clapping him genially on the back the president exclaimed:

"Go and talk to your wife, old man. You've left her alone long enough."

"All right—I will," replied the gambler, not sorry of any excuse to get away.

Mr. Parker waited till he was out of hearing, then, leaning quickly over to his companion, he exclaimed in a tense whisper:

"Steell, I need your help."

The lawyer looked at him in surprise. Removing his cigar from his mouth he said:

"My help? By all means. What can I do for you?"

Mr. Parker gave a quick glance behind him to see if they were observed, and then he said:

"My God, Steell, something terrible has happened! At any cost, we mustn't let the wife know—"

The lawyer stared at his companion in amazement.

"What is it, for Heaven's sake?" he demanded, looking anxiously at his *vis-a-vis*.

"The diamonds are lost!" replied Parker hoarsely.

"The diamonds lost!"

"Yes—lost—he has returned without them. They went down in the *Abyssinia*. At least, that's what he says—"

The lawyer started.

"You think—"

"I think nothing," replied the president cautiously. "I want to know. That's why I want you to help me—to find out—you understand?"

The lawyer nodded:

"Some detective work, eh?"

"Precisely. The stones may have gone down to the bottom of the ocean, or they may not. For all we know the ship may have been set on fire purposely, in order to create such a panic—"

The lawyer protested.

"Surely you don't think Kenneth—"

The president shook his head.

"I accuse nobody. I want to find out."

He was silent for a moment, and then after a pause he went on:

"I suppose you've heard, as well as everybody else, how Traynor has been plunging in Wall Street recently."

The lawyer nodded. Hesitatingly he replied:

"Yes—I have. Unfortunately, the reports are true. Investigations I have conducted privately on my own account have convinced me that Kenneth has been a big plunger for some time. But as far as I know, he has operated only within his means. I have often remonstrated with him about the folly of it, but he enjoys the excitement of the speculation game, and as long as he kept within bounds and gambled with his own money I didn't see that anyone had any right to interfere."

"Ah, just so—as long as he operated with his own means and with his own money. But suppose the market suddenly goes against such a man, and he is face to face with a tremendous loss, possibly ruin, what does such a man do nine times out of ten?"

"Blow his brains out."

"Yes—sometimes that, but often he succumbs to temptation, and takes what isn't his—"

"Then you think that Kenneth—"

"I think nothing. I want to know. He has come back from Africa a changed man. He is surly, morose, secretive. That man has something on his conscience. We must find out what it is. It is up to you to ferret it out. Set your detectives to work. The company will spend the last cent in its treasury to find those stones. You must trail his associates, find out where he goes. The diamonds are probably right here in New York. Who first took Kenneth to Wall Street?"

"Signor Keralio—"

"Ah—always that fellow! Who is he?"

"An adventurer of the worst type. I have had him shadowed by one of my men. He has a police record as a dangerous criminal of international reputation."

"And Kenneth's valet—that fellow Francois."

"He was formerly in Keralio's employ."

The President rose. Extending his hand to the lawyer, he said:

"That's enough. I don't think the trail will be hard to pick up. Spare no expense. Good night!"

CHAPTER XV

The last guest had gone. One by one the lights in the Traynor residence were extinguished. The servants, tired after an exciting and strenuous day, had gone to their quarters.

In the hall downstairs, the grandfather's clock rang out its musical chimes and then, in ponderous tones, slowly struck the twelve hours of midnight.

The master of the house was sitting at the desk in the library, looking over some papers. From time to time he glanced significantly, first at the clock and then at the corner where Helen and Ray were chatting over the events of the day. At last the young girl took the hint. Jumping up, she exclaimed good naturedly:

"How selfish I am to be sitting gossiping here when poor Kenneth is so tired. Go to bed, both of you. I'm so sleepy myself I can hardly keep awake. Good night!"

"Good night, dear!" said Helen, rising and kissing her.

"Good night, Ken! Pleasant dreams," cried the young girl as she left the room.

"Good night!" he responded hoarsely.

The sound of her footsteps died away in the distance and Helen and the gambler sat there in silence. He watched her

Arthur Hornblow

furtively, trying to guess the trend of her thoughts, his eyes bloodshot with wine, feasting on every line of her girlish figure.

Never had she looked more beautiful, more desirable, than this evening. Her *decollete* gown revealed a white, plump neck, her lips were red and tempting, her large dark eyes fairly sparkled from excitement. It was a vision to distract a saint and Handsome was no saint. It was indeed only with the greatest difficulty that he curbed his impatience to carry off the prize that lay within his grasp.

"Are you tired," he said at last. "Do you want to go to bed?"

"Not very," she answered. "I'm too excited to sleep. Hasn't it been an exciting day?"

He made no reply, pretending to be occupied at the desk, and she relapsed into a dream silence, glad of a few quiet, peaceful moments to be alone with her thoughts. How good it was to have him home again! Now she could be at peace once more and enjoy life as she used to. She could go to the opera, to the theater. The days would not be so monotonous. She wondered why she was still unable to shake off the feeling of anxiety and apprehension which had haunted her ever since he went away. With a devoted husband safe at her side, what reason had she for feeling depressed? Yet, for some reason she was unable to explain, she was not able even now to throw off her melancholy and presentiment of danger.

There recurred to her mind what Signor Keralio had said, his veiled, ambiguous words of warning. Could it be true, was it possible that her husband had deceived her all these years and unsuspected by her, had led a double life of deceit and disloyalty? Certainly there was much that needed explanation. The loss of the diamonds did not directly concern her, although she felt that, too, was part of the mystery. But his strange aloofness of manner, his inexplicable loss of memory and nervousness, the frenzied outburst when she had mentioned Keralio's name that afternoon, the sudden craving for drink—was not all this to some extent, corroboration of what the fencing master has told her? She thought she would question him, speak to him openly, frankly, as a loyal wife should the man she loves, and give him an opportunity to explain. Now was as good a time as ever. Looking up she said abruptly:

"Signor Keralio was here while you were away. I started telling you this afternoon, but you got so excited—"

Making a deprecatory gesture with his hand he said indifferently:

"That's all right. I was tired and nervous. I'm quieter now. What did Keralio have to say?"

"Nothing worth listening to. He never says anything but impertinences."

He shrugged his shoulders.

"You mustn't take him too seriously."

Hotly she retorted:

"He takes himself too seriously. If he only knew how repellent he is to a decent woman he would cease to annoy me."

He laughed.

"Oh, Keralio's not a bad sort—when you get to know him. Those foreigners think nothing of making love to a woman—"

"I don't want to know him," she retorted with spirit, "and what's more, I don't want him coming here. One evening he was so insulting that I had to show him the door. He had the impudence to come again. So I had my servant put him out. You won't invite him here again, will you?"

He was silent, while she sat watching him, amazed that he did not at once fiercely resent the insult done her in his absence. After a pause, he said awkwardly:

"I don't invite him. Keralio's the kind of a chap who invites himself."

"But can't you put him out?" she demanded with growing irritation.

"No—I can't," he answered doggedly.

"Why?" she demanded firmly.

"I can't—that's all!"

She looked at him wonderingly, and the color came and went in her face and neck. There was a note almost of contempt in her voice as she demanded:

"What is the hold this creature has on you? Is it something you are ashamed of?"

The blood surged to his face and the veins stood out on his temples like whipcord. Another instant and it had receded, leaving him ghastly pale.

"We have business interests in common, that's all," he said hastily and apologetically. "He has been very useful to me. I don't like him any more than you do, but in business one can't criticize too closely the manners or morals of one's associates."

"No, but a man can prevent his associates from annoying his wife."

He made no answer, but toyed nervously with a paper cutter. Determined to get at the truth, she went on:

"What business interests can you have together? Is it legitimate business or merely stock gambling?"

"What do you mean?"

Rising from the divan, she went toward him. Earnestly, she said:

"Kenneth, I've wanted to speak to you about this matter for a long time. During your absence I've heard rumors. Things have been insinuated. A hint has been dropped here, gossip has been overheard there—all to the effect that you are heavily involved in Wall Street. Is it true?"

For a moment he was silent, at a loss what to answer. He could not imagine the reason for the questioning or where it might lead him, but instinct warned him that it was dangerous ground and that caution was necessary. Why hadn't Francois told him of his brother's Wall Street operations? It would never do to show himself entirely ignorant of them. If such rumors existed, there was probably some basis of them. No doubt his brother had played the market and kept from his wife the extent of his losses.

"Is it true?" she repeated.

He shrugged his shoulders. Nonchalantly, he replied:

"Never believe all you hear!"

Her face lit up with pleasure.

"Really?" she exclaimed. "It isn't true?"

"Not a word of it. I have money invested in stocks and bonds, but anyone who accuses me of wild cat speculation is guilty of telling what I would very politely call a d—d lie!"

Reassured more by his ease and carelessness of manner than by his actual words of denial, the young wife gave an exclamation of delight.

"Oh, I'm so glad!" she exclaimed. "You've no idea how relieved I feel. It was worrying me terribly to feel that you might be in difficulties and had not thought enough of me to take me into your confidence." Looking at him appealingly she added:

"You will always confide in me, won't you Ken?"

"Sure I will, sweetheart—"

Trembling with the ardor he was trying to control he seized hold of her hand and drew her on to his knee. She offered no resistance, but passively sat there, clasped against his broad shoulder, her face radiant with happiness at the load which his words had taken off her mind.

Putting his arm round her waist, he leaned forward as if to kiss her, but drawing quickly back she said:

"There's still something else I must ask you before my happiness is quite complete."

"What's that?" he demanded, impatient at these continual interruptions to his amorous advances.

Turning she looked steadily into his face, as if trying to read the truth or falsity of his answer. She could not see his eyes, veiled as they were by the glasses, but that sensitive mouth she knew so well, that determined chin, that high forehead crowned by the bushy brown hair with its solitary white lock—all these were as dear to her as they had always been. To think that he might have fondled some other woman as he was now fondling her was intolerable agony.

"Kenneth," she said slowly and impressively, "are you sure that there is no part of your life that you have kept hidden from me?"

He started and for a moment changed color. What did she mean? Was it possible that she suspected the substitution, or was she alluding to some past history of his brother's life, of which he knew nothing? Evasively, he answered:

"Why all these question, sweetheart, the first day I come home. Is this the kind of welcome you promised me, the one I had a right to expect. I am very tired. Let us go to bed."

His arm still around her, he again drew her to him and, stooping, tried to reach her mouth with his own. But again she resisted, her mind too disturbed by jealousy to be in a mood to respond to his wooing. Gently she said:

"I know you are tired, Ken. I am tired, too,—tired of all these rumors and slanderous insinuations. I have been made unhappy by hearing this gossip. It is my right to tell you what I have heard and ask for a straightforward, loyal explanation. I know you are true to me. I have never doubted it for an instant. I only want a word from you to forget what I've heard and dismiss the matter from my mind forever."

He looked at her, an amused kind of expression playing about the corners of his mouth. It was only with an effort that he controlled the muscles of his face. What a comedy, he thought to himself! Here was this sweet little woman breaking her heart over something which, as far as he knew, didn't exist. But he must continue to play his part, no matter at what cost. Evidently, she had heard something for which there might be some basis of truth. She might even have proofs of his brother's infidelity, and ready to produce them. Too sweeping a denial might still further complicate matters, arouse suspicion, and end in exposure. Cautiously, he replied:

"You know all there is in my life, sweetheart. I never conceal anything from you."

Looking searchingly at him, she demanded:

Arthur Hornblow

"Never?"

"Never."

"Has there been another woman in your life, Kenneth, since you married me?"

"No, sweetheart—never. If anyone told you that or even insinuated it, he was a scoundrel. It's a damned lie! You are and always will be the only one—"

Her head fell back on his shoulder.

"Then I am completely happy!" she murmured.

His arms folded about her and she felt his warm breath on her cheek. But this time she did not resist. It felt good to be sheltered there in those strong arms against the attacks and calumnies of the world.

"It is late," he murmured.

Suddenly, he threw her head back and bending down till his mouth reached hers he kissed her full on the lips. She did not resist, but just abandoned herself, responding only feebly to the fierce passion that made him tremble like a leaf. His face flushed, his hands shaking, he murmured:

"It is very late. Are you not tired?"

"No dear—I'm not tired. There's no hurry. We needn't get up early to-morrow. It's so beautiful here—sitting together like this—so happy in each other's company."

"But I am tired," he said, trying to control his emotion.

It was almost more than he could endure, yet still he mastered himself, and resisted the temptation that arose violently within him to take her by force, if needs be, and carry her into the inner room, as the wild beast, tiring of playing with its victim, suddenly ends the game by seizing its hapless prey and drags it away to its lair. Was he not the master? Why should he allow her childish prattle to stand in the way of his desires. For years, Handsome had not known female society save that of those wretched outcasts who infest the mining camps. He had caroused with them and quarreled with them. He had even loved one of them—after the rough and ready fashion of the *veldt*. She was a Spaniard, a tall handsome woman, with large black eyes and the temper of a fury. She had killed her husband in a drunken brawl, and on leaving prison had gone to South Africa. She met the gambler one night in a gambling house, and, without as much as asking for an introduction, she went up to him and, in a characteristic Spanish style, gave him a hearty kiss on both cheeks. It was her way of notifying her female associates that, henceforth, the big miner was her man. Handsome accepted the challenge, and for a couple of years they lived as happily together as can two adventurers who are in constant hot water with the police. One day, in a fit of drunken jealousy, she struck him. Furious with rage, he seized her by the neck. He did not mean to harm her; it was his giant strength that was to blame. Anyhow her neck was broken and the coroner called it an accident. For a week or so, Handsome was really sorry. She was the only woman he had ever cared for. She at least was a woman.

But this slip of a girl, with her childish prattle and aristocratic airs, was quite different. Accustomed to the rougher ways of the camp, her fine manners and refined graces at first had rather intimidated him. He did not feel at home with her. He felt awkward and ill at ease. Yet, for all that, she was a woman, too—a woman of his own race, desirable, tempting. When Francois had first suggested that he impersonate his brother and enjoy his fortune, he had said nothing about his brother's wife. Perhaps he reserved her for his master, Keralio. At the thought, a pang of jealousy went through him. If Keralio, why not he? Evidently Keralio had been stalking the game, for she complained of his conduct and had dismissed him from the house. Yet, in what position was he to frustrate Keralio in any of his schemes? He had him in his power; he was completely at his mercy. He allowed him to masquerade in New York as the millionaire, but he was the real master of the Traynor home. Even now, Francois might be spying on their actions, eager to report to the arch conspirator. Rising from the chair, he lifted her to her feet.

"Come, darling—it is late—"

He led her slowly, almost imperceptibly, in the direction of the inner room. A feeling of languor came over her, and she allowed him to lead her, abandoning herself to his ardent, feverish embrace, responding every now and then to the hot kisses he rained on her mouth and neck. Through her thin dress he could feel her soft form pressing against him. From her neck arose a delicious aroma, a kind of feminine incense that still further aroused and lashed his desire.

"I adore you—I adore you!" he murmured, as he kissed her again. Slowly he led her past the bookcase and marble Venus to the open door of her pink and white boudoir.

She looked up at him in surprise.

"How you love me!" she murmured. "You never used to care for me like this."

Her head on his shoulder, her eyes half closed, she was conscious only of the presence of the man she loved better than anyone in the world.

Yet even now, in the hour of her supreme content and felicity, when all her tormenting anxieties and doubts had been dissipated by his frank words of denial, there was still something that worried her. He was changed somehow, even in his love making. It was delicious to be loved passionately, fiercely, like this—to be carried off by force, as it were, by your own husband. But she did not understand how a man could change so much in a few weeks. Kenneth had always loved her deeply, but never had she known him display such ardor as this. She had heard that men change, particularly after long absences from home. Some, she had heard, became colder; others were more demonstrative. Of the two, she thought the latter preferable. If there was such love in the world, why should it not be shown her. Her own temperament was cold, but no woman could but feel flattered that she possessed the power to arouse men to such passion.

At last they had reached the threshold of the boudoir. What to him was an earthly paradise, was almost attained. In a state of blissful helplessness, intoxicated by a delicious sensation of being completely dominated by a will stronger than her own, she permitted him to take her where he wished. Her eyes closed, her head on his shoulder, she submitted willingly to his fervent kisses. Another moment and he had closed the door behind them, when, suddenly, a commotion on the landing outside the library aroused both with a start. There was the sound of voices and people running up the stairs.

"What's that?" exclaimed Helen startled.

Irritated at this unlooked for interruption, the gambler went quickly toward the landing to investigate. Francois met him at the library door. In his hand he held an envelope. Holding it out, he said:

"A telegram for Madame!"

"A telegram!" cried Helen, rushing forward. "Good God, I hope Dorothy is not—"

She tore it open, while Handsome stood by in silence. On the valet's face there was a triumphant expression, the gratified smile of one rogue who enjoys the discomfiture of another.

Helen suddenly gave a cry.

"It's as I thought!" she exclaimed. "Dorothy is worse. The

Arthur Hornblow

doctor thinks it is scarlet fever. I must go to her at once."

"Go where?" demanded Handsome in consternation.

"To Philadelphia."

"To Philadelphia to-night?" he cried in dismay.

"Yes—to-night," she said firmly.

He protested vigorously.

"Nonsense—you can't go to-night. It will do no good. Wait till the morning. There are no trains."

Quickly, the valet drew from his pocket a time-table. With a side glance at his master, he said:

"There is a train at 1.15. If Madame is quick, she will make it. The car is already waiting downstairs."

Helen seized her fur coat, which the obliging valet had also brought up from the hall.

"Yes—yes. Throw a few things in my bag. You needn't come, Ken. I'll telephone you directly I get to Philadelphia. Good-bye!"

The next instant she was gone and the gambler, with a muttered curse, went to the sideboard and poured out a glass of whiskey, with which to drown his disappointment.

CHAPTER XVI

For a person so fastidious and particular, so fond of the luxurious and the elegant, Signor Keralio had certainly selected a queer neighborhood for his abode. Miles distant from the fashionable centers, far away up in the Bronx, he occupied the entire top floor of a dingy, broken down tenement. There were no other people in the house, it being in such bad repair that no one cared to live in it, and as Keralio paid as much as all the previous tenants combined and made no requests for improvements, the landlord was only too glad to leave him undisturbed. It was situated at the extreme end of a blind alley and, there being no egress from the street save at one end, there was consequently little or no traffic and, for the great part of the day and night, the silence was as deep and unbroken as in the open country.

With his neighbors Signor Keralio was distantly polite, but never intimate. The district was a poor one, being settled mostly by Italian laborers who rose and went to bed with the sun and toiled too long and too hard each day to bother their heads as to why such a fine gentleman as the Signor appeared to be, should live in such squalid quarters. No one had ever been admitted to his flat. If the baker called, he left the bread on the mat; if a chance peddler or book agent happened to wander in, he had to talk through closed doors. The Signor was always busy and could not be disturbed. The lights often burned all night long, and sometimes people drove up in a taxi and went away again. For a while the corner gossips speculated idly as to who he might be, but gradually they lost all interest.

Arthur Hornblow

When he purchased trifles at the corner grocery he gave out casually that he was a newspaper man and had to work all night, and the fact that muffled sounds of hammering and machinery in motion had been heard at all hours, only helped to make the explanation more plausible.

To-night, Keralio was perhaps more anxious than at any time to discourage callers—especially should they happen to be inquisitive secret service agents. Another few days and he would have nothing more to fear. The presses would soon have completed their work and $500,000 worth of as fine a $10 counterfeit as ever deceived a bank teller would be ready for distribution. Half of them had already been run off and, as he held them up to the light and critically examined the silken thread that ran here and there through the specially prepared paper and noted the careful coloring, the beautifully geometrical lathe work and skilfully traced signatures, he silently congratulated himself. Here was half a million dollars' worth of splendid currency. Detection was absolutely impossible. Had not Francois already succeeded in passing a lot? After all had been disposed of, he could afford to take a rest. On the proceeds of this rich haul, he could live like a prince for a few years in Europe, and when that was all gone, he still had the diamonds to fall back upon. Glancing at the clock, he wondered why Handsome did not come. He was anxious to get possession of the diamonds. It was too soon to attempt doing anything with the stones now. The hue and cry would be too loud. All the diamond markets would be watched, if they were not already. He had a suspicion that Parker and Steell suspected something wrong. Francois had seen the President in earnest consultation with the lawyer directly after Handsome had announced the loss. He had not been able to hear what was said, but from their manner he inferred that the diamonds were the sole subject of conversation. They did not question Handsome's identity. That never entered their heads, but they doubted his story of losing the stones. They, no doubt, thought he had used the diamonds to make good Wall Street losses.

He chuckled as he thought how admirably his scheme had worked out. He had hinted at Kenneth being heavily short in this street, which at once explained a motive for Kenneth diverting the stones to his own use. Yes, he had triumphed over them all—except one. Helen Traynor, so far, had foiled him in everything, and the more she resisted and insulted him, the more determined he was to drag her at his feet. Handsome, poor devil, fondly imagined he would inherit the wife as well as the fortune. How could he guess that he, Keralio, would send a bogus telegram just in time to dash the cup from his lips.

Impatiently he strode up and down the rooms. Why was Handsome late? A frown darkened his face. He had better not trifle with him. He must obey without question or take the consequences. He was in no mood to be defied.

Suddenly, he started and listened. His alert ear had caught the sound of approaching footsteps on the stairs outside. A moment later came three deliberate knocks on the door, a signal which indicated a friendly visitor. Quickly, Keralio went forward and withdrew the bolt.

Francois entered, suit case in hand. Hardly before he could take breath after the long climb, Keralio exclaimed:

"Well, how are they going?"

The Frenchman grinned.

"*A merveille*! Like hot cakes. I've passed all of zem. Good work, is it not?"

"And the real stuff?" demanded Keralio.

"Is in here."

The valet pointed to the leather case.

Eagerly Keralio seized the portmanteau, and, opening it, emptied the contents. A perfect shower of greenbacks—genuine ones this time—fell upon the floor. With shaking hands, like a miser who trembles as he handles his hoarded gold, Keralio picked up the money by armfuls and, taking it to a table, proceeded to count it.

"Is it all here?" he demanded suspiciously.

The valet scowled.

"Do you think I'm holding any back on you? *Ma foi, non!*"

Keralio, still counting, fixed his assistant with steely, piercing eyes.

"No, Francois, I think you know me too well for that. You know I never forget a service; you also know I never forgive anyone who crosses my will."

The valet shrugged his shoulders. In an injured tone he asked:

"What's all ze talk about? I work well for you. I do your dirty work, *n'est ce pas?* I never complain—I am faithful. What more would you have?"

"Why should you complain? You get your share," rejoined his chief sternly.

The valet was silent and Keralio went on:

"A few days more and we'll be rid of all the new stuff. Then we'll take down the presses and carry away the parts, piece by piece. When we're ready to leave this hole, there won't be a shred of evidence left. Have you heard any news from our man in Washington? What are the secret service men doing?"

"Ze alarm is given. Zey have spotted several of ze bills. Half a dozen of ze cleverest sleuths in ze country have been put on our trail. Zey will not succeed. Ze scent is cold. We've got zem completely doped."

Keralio looked anxious.

"Is there any danger of them having shadowed you and followed you here?"

"No—*mon cher, pas le mains du monde*. It took me three hours to come here from ze Pennsylvania station—such a crazy in and out route I gave ze chauffeur. If they succeed in following such a labyrinth as that, they deserve to get us."

Keralio smiled and pointed to a bottle of brandy on the table. Approvingly, he said:

"Good boy! There, take a drink and a cigar—"

After the valet had refreshed himself, he again confronted his chief.

"What else *a votre service*?"

Keralio pointed carelessly to a seat. In a commanding tone, he said:

"Yes—I have more work for you. Sit down. I will tell you."

The valet took a chair and waited. Keralio looked at him meditatively for a moment. Then suddenly he asked:

"When did you leave the house?"

"This afternoon at three o'clock."

"When did Mrs. Traynor return from Philadelphia?"

"Yesterday—furious at the hoax played upon her? Miss Dorothy is perfectly well—"

Keralio smiled.

"Of course. I sent that telegram."

The valet grinned. Admiringly, he exclaimed:

"You are admirable! *Quel homme, mon dieu, quel homme!*"

Paying no heed to the compliment, Keralio went on:

"What did Handsome say?"

"He is puzzled himself and can't understand. Everyone's up in the air. They think it is a discharged maid who did it for spite."

"The next time Mrs. Traynor receives a sudden message about her baby it will not be a hoax."

The valet looked up in surprise.

"What do you mean?"

Keralio did not answer the question immediately, but sat nervously twisting his fingers, a moody sullen look in his pale saturnine face. At last, breaking the heavy silence, he said:

"That woman insulted me. You saw it. You were there—"

The valet nodded.

"You mean she put you out—ah, *oui*, she has a *diable* of a temper when angry."

Keralio nodded.

"Yes—that I can never forgive. She shall ask my pardon on her knees. I will break her spirit, humiliate her pride. I have been taxing my brain how to do it. At last I have hit on a plan—one that cannot fail and you shall help me."

"In what way *s'il vous plait?*"

Bending forward, his black eyes flashing, Keralio said earnestly:

"That woman is devoted to only two beings in this world—her husband and her baby. Sooner or later, perhaps only in a few days, she will discover that Handsome is an impostor. He is such a fool that exposure is inevitable. The blow will almost kill her. Above all, it will humiliate her pride to know that unwittingly she has allowed that drunken brute, that poor counterfeit of her husband, to caress and fondle her. Next in her affections comes her baby. If any danger threatened the child, she would stop at nothing, she would make any sacrifice to ward off the danger. I propose to bring about just that situation—"

The valet half started up from his chair. Hardened and callous as he was in crime, he was hardly prepared to go to that extreme.

"Death?" he exclaimed, horror stricken, "you would kill ze child?"

"No fool—not kill the child. I'll kidnap it—that's all. We'll bring the child here and, then I'll write the mother, telling her where it is and to come to it, but warning her that if she values the child's life, she must tell no one, and must come here unaccompanied. Once she is here, I will take care of the rest. Do you understand?"

The valet breathed more freely.

"So you will that I—"

His chief nodded.

"Precisely. You'll take the flyer to Philadelphia. Say you come

Arthur Hornblow

from the mother. They'll have no suspicion. Take the child and come here at once. Understand?"

"*Oui*, monsieur."

Keralio rose. In commanding tones, he said:

"Then go at once."

The valet went to get his hat. As he approached the door Keralio halted him and said:

"What's Handsome doing—keeping sober?"

"He has to, for I lock up all ze liquor. He lives like a lord, buying swell clothes, riding in ze automobile. Last night he lost at ze club $10,000 he had drew from ze bank."

Keralio gave a low whistle.

"The deuce he did! Living high, eh? Well—that's all right. Let him enjoy it. His gay life won't last long—only just as long as it suits my purpose."

"Hush! Not a word—here he is!"

From the landing outside came the sound of a heavy body lurching. Then came the noise of someone groping for the handle, followed by a furious pounding on the wooden panels.

"Open up there, will you!" shouted a hoarse voice.

"Drunk, as usual!" said Keralio contemptuously.

He suddenly threw the door open and the gambler, burly and unsteady on his legs, almost fell in. He was in evening dress, his collar and tie rumpled, his hair unkempt. His face was flushed, his eyes bloodshot. Reeling in, he hiccoughed:

"What'n h—ll do you live so far up town for? I thought I'd never get here. Say, this is the end of the world, ain't it? Jumping off place, eh? Stopped several times on the way to get a drink. My cabby nearly got lost. Been driving me round for three hours trying to locate the blooming house. Charged me $5. Hell of a good business, ain't it. Tain't on the level to treat an old pal that way. Y'oughter be ashamed o' yourself."

"I'm more ashamed of you—for making such a beast of yourself," rejoined Keralio angrily. "Stop your cursed noise or you'll have the police on top of us!"

Without ceremony, he pushed the newcomer into a seat and made a gesture to Francois to go. The valet went toward the door.

"Remember," said Keralio warningly. "There must be no blundering. I want the child brought here—"

"*Oui*, monsieur—it shall be as you say."

The door closed and Keralio turned quietly to the miner. Sternly, and in a manner that brooked no nonsense, he demanded:

"Did you bring the diamonds?"

Handsome grinned, and pointed to his waist.

"I've got 'em all right!" With another hiccough, he added: "But there's no hurry, old sport. Let's have a drink before we get talking business."

In two rapid strides Keralio was up to him. Fiercely he said:

"Give me the stones—give me them I say. We've no time for your d—d fooling. Hand them over. Come—"

For a moment the gambler just sat and looked at his master. A giant in physical strength compared with the slightly built foreigner, he could have overpowered him as a child might crush an egg-shell, but he lacked the mentality, the magnetism of the Italian. He was cowed, dominated by the stronger mind. Grumbling, he began to fumble at his waist:

"I don't see what's the hurry."

"But I see," exclaimed Keralio, his eyes growing larger, as he already saw the colossal stones glittering in his hand.

The next instant Handsome had slid his hand under his waist-coat and unbuckled a belt he wore next his shirt. Unfastening a pocket and taking out the contents, he growled:

"Here they are! I'm glad to get rid of the d—d things."

With a cry of exultant joy Keralio took hold of the stones and, going to the window, greedily feasted his eyes on them. Report had not exaggerated the value and extraordinary beauty of the gems. They were worth more than a million.

"What do I get out of it?" whined the gambler.

Keralio regarded him with contempt. Dryly he said:

"You get out of it that you're not sitting in the electric chair for murdering your twin brother. You get out of it that you're playing the role of the millionaire, basking in the smiles of your brother's charming wife, and making a drunken beast of yourself—that's what you get out of it. Isn't it enough?"

Handsome winced. Keralio had a direct way of saying things to which there was no answer possible.

"All right," he grumbled, "I'm not kicking."

"No—I wouldn't if I were you."

Changing the topic, Keralio carelessly lit a cigarette and, between the puffs, asked:

"How's your wife?"

"My wife? You mean his wife?"

Keralio smiled.

"Yours—for the time being."

Handsome scowled.

"It isn't so easy as I thought," he replied. "I don't know if she suspects something's wrong or not, but ever since that evening she was called to Philadelphia she avoids me like the pest. I can see in her face that she's puzzled. 'It's my husband, and yet not my husband'—that's what she's thinking all the time. I can guess her thoughts by the expression on her face."

Keralio shrugged his shoulders.

"That's your own fault. I gave you the opportunity. You failed to profit by it. You got drunk the first night you arrived. Kenneth Traynor was a temperate man. Is it no wonder you excited wonder and talk? Then you were stupid under questionning and gave equivocal answers. Your explanation to Parker about the diamonds was more than unfortunate; it was idiotic. His suspicions were at once aroused. He may yet give us trouble before we have time to get rid of the stones. Finding the wife eluded you, you began to stay out late at night. You caroused, you drank hard, you gambled—all of which follies your brother never committed. In other words, you are a fool."

The miner pointed to the diamonds which still lay on the table. Sulkily he asked:

"Is that all you wanted?"

Keralio put the gems away in his pocket, and pointed to the stacks of newly printed counterfeit money that lay in stacks all over the floor.

"No, you can help me make up bundles of this stuff."

Handsome opened wide his eyes at sight of the crisp currency. Greedily he exclaimed:

"Say—that's some money! Ain't they beauties?"

Keralio made an impatient gesture and, taking off his coat, made a gesture to his companion to do likewise.

"Come—there's no time to talk. We must get rid of it all before morning. For all I know the detectives may be watching the house now."

CHAPTER XVII

"I'm sure it was Mary," exclaimed Ray positively. "I never did like the girl. She was sullen and vicious and would stop at nothing to get even with us for discharging her."

"Perhaps you are right," said Helen, "although it is hard to believe that a woman would do such a cruel thing to a mother. Just imagine how worried I was all the way to Philadelphia, only to find when I got there that no message had been sent, and Dorothy was perfectly well."

It was evening. The two women were sitting alone in the library on the second floor, Ray busy at her trousseau, Helen helping her with a piece of embroidery. The master of the house was absent, as usual. He had not come home to dinner, having telephoned at the last minute that he was detained at the club, a thing of such common occurrence since his return from South Africa that Helen had come to accept it as a matter of course. Indeed, things had come to such a pass that she rather welcomed his absence. She preferred the sweet, amiable companionship of her little sister to that of a man who had suddenly become exacting, over-bearing and quarrelsome.

"Why don't you let Dorothy come home?" asked Ray. "Then you wouldn't have this constant worry about her."

"I think I will, now that we are more settled and things are quieter. I wrote to auntie to-day that I might go to Philadelphia one day next week to bring her home. You are right. I shall not be happy until she's with me. I have such terrible dreams about her. If anything were to happen that child, I think it would kill me."

Ray nodded approvingly. Sympathetically, she said:

"Yes, dear. You'll feel better satisfied when she's with you. Besides she'll be a companion for you—especially when I'm married—"

Helen sighed and turned away her face so her sister should not see the tears that suddenly filled her eyes. Sorrowfully, she said:

"It will be terrible to lose you, dear. Of course, I'm happy over your marriage. It would be very selfish in me to want to stand in the way of your happiness. I'm sure I wish you and Wilbur every joy imaginable. But I shall certainly feel very lonely when you are gone."

The young girl looked closely at her sister. She realized that her sister was no longer the happy, contented woman she once was, and she readily guessed the cause. Helen had not taken her into her confidence, but she had ears and eyes. Living in the house in such close intimacy, she could not help noticing that the relations between the wife and husband were no longer what they had been. Guardedly she said:

"But you have Kenneth."

Helen sighed and was silent.

Ray looked up. More gently she said:

"Haven't you your husband, dear?"

Her sister shook her head. There was a note of utter discouragement and melancholy in her voice as she answered:

"He is seldom home—his club seems to have more attraction

for him. I rarely see him except at breakfast time." She was silent for a moment, and then added quickly: "Would you believe that he hasn't been home a single night since the time I was called to Philadelphia?"

Ray opened her eyes.

"He's out all night?"

"Yes—all night. The other morning it was seven o'clock when he came home—and his dress suit and shirt looked as if he had been in a fight."

The young girl put down her work and looked at her sister in dismay.

"Sis!—what's the matter with Ken all at once?"

Helen made no reply, but covering her face with her two hands, burst into tears. Ray rose quickly and going over to where she was sitting, sat on the edge of the chair and put her arms about her. Soothingly she said:

"Don't cry, dear, don't cry. He will soon be himself again. His terrible experience on the steamer upset him dreadfully. His nervous system underwent such a shock that it has entirely changed his character. Wilbur says it is quite a common phenomenon. Only the other day he read in some medical book an article on that very subject. The writer says any great shock of that kind can cause a temporary disarrangement of the moral sense and perceptions. For example, a man who, under ordinary circumstances is a perfect model of a husband, with every good quality and virtue, may suddenly lose all sense of conduct and become am unprincipled *roue*. In other words, we have two natures within us. When our system is working normally we succeed in keeping the evil that's in us under control; but following any great shock, the system is disarranged, the evil gains the ascendancy, and we appear quite another person. This explains the dual personality about which

Wilbur and I had an argument the other day. Don't you remember?"

Helen nodded. Sadly she said:

"I begin to think you are right. Certainly he has changed. If he had been like this when I first met him I should never have married him. It is not the Kenneth I learned to love." Bitterly, she added: "As he is now, I feel I dislike and detest him. Unless he soon changes for the better, I shall leave him. In self respect I can't go on living like this?"

Kissing her sister again, Ray rose and went back to her seat. Confidently, she said:

"Don't worry, dear. I'm sure everything will be all right soon. You see if I'm not right. By my wedding day—only three weeks away now—you'll think as much of Ken as ever—"

"I hope so, dear, but three weeks is a long time to wait—"

The young girl laughed.

"Why that's nothing at all. Just imagine Ken is ill or gone away from you on a visit for that length of time—"

As she spoke the door opened, and Francois entered with a silver salver, which he presented to his mistress.

"A letter for Madame."

Helen looked at the envelope and threw it down with a gesture of impatience. Crossly, she exclaimed:

"Francois, I do wish you'd be more careful. Can't you read. Don't you see the letter is addressed to Mr. Traynor?"

The valet nodded.

"*Oui*, madame. But as Monsieur is out I thought that possibly madame—"

Incensed more at the fellow's impudent air than by what he actually said, Helen lost her temper. Angrily, she exclaimed:

"Don't think. People of your class are not hired to think; they are paid to do as they are told. You've been very careless in your work recently. The next time it happens I shall have to tell you to find another place."

The valet smiled. An insolent look passed over his sallow, angular face. Dropping completely his deferential manner and fixing the two women with a bold, familiar stare, he said impudently:

"You needn't wait till next time. I'll quit right now, *parbleu*. It's a rotten job, anyhow."

Indignant, Helen pointed to the door.

"Go!" she cried. "The housekeeper will settle with you. Never let me see your face again."

The Frenchman shrugged his shoulders and went toward the door. As he reached it, he turned round, a sneer on his face:

"You'll see me again all right, but ze circumstances may be different? My lady may not be so proud ze next time."

With this parting shot, he went away, and a moment later they heard him going up to his room to pack his things.

Ray turned to her sister. Reprovingly, she said:

"Weren't you a little severe with him?"

Helen shook her head. Quickly, she said:

Arthur Hornblow

"I never could bear the sight of the man. He is treacherous and deceitful. I'm not at all sure that he's honest. It was only after he'd been here some time that I learned he was formerly with Signor Keralio. That was enough to set me against him. Like master, like valet, as the saying goes, and it's usually a true saying. On several occasions lately I have noticed things that seemed suspicious. The fellow is more intimate now with Kenneth than I, his wife, have ever been. Only the other day I discovered them in earnest and intimate conversation. Directly I appeared they separated and Francois, instead of continuing to converse on terms of apparent social equality, was once more the fawning valet. I didn't take the trouble to ask Kenneth what it all meant. So many singular things have happened since his return, that this only adds one more to the list."

"May I come in?" said a voice.

Helen looked up quickly. It was Wilbur Steell who was standing at the door with his head half in the room, laughing at them. The two women had been so busy talking that they had not heard the sound of approaching footsteps. With an exclamation of joy Ray jumped to her feet and ran up to him.

"It's Wilbur—my precious Wilbur!"

Helen nodded approvingly, as she noticed the girl's enthusiasm. Certainly her sister had changed. She was hardly the cold, self-centered Ray of six months ago. With a smile she said:

"It's astonishing how a man can alter a girl—if he's the right kind."

The lawyer laughed.

"It works both ways. The right kind of woman can make a man change his ways—even a hardened old bachelor. Who could have guessed that I would ever fall in love?"

Helen sighed.

"What is love? We have it to-day; it eludes us to-morrow. A few weeks ago I thought I loved my husband better than any being in the world. To-day, I can hardly look him in the face. How do you account for it?"

Dropping into a chair, the lawyer look serious.

"I can't account for it, nor can I blame you. Kenneth has returned from South Africa a changed man. Whether the wreck and the loss of the diamonds affected his mind I do not know. Only a psychologist could determine that. But he is not the same. Where is he to-night?"

Helen threw up her hands.

"Do I ever know?" she exclaimed wearily. "I haven't seen him since morning, and don't expect to see him before breakfast to-morrow. He's at his club or drinking and carousing, or in some gambling house playing roulette. How do I know?"

"It is certainly a most singular case," said the lawyer meditatively. "Mr. Parker and I have gone carefully over his accounts at the Company's office. Everything is perfectly regular. There only remains the missing diamonds. We have detectives working on half a dozen clues but so far we have accomplished nothing. We have also gone to Washington to get the secret service men interested in the case on the ground that if the diamonds are here they were smuggled in and no duty was paid. But we found the secret service men busy following up counterfeiters. The country is being flooded with counterfeit $10 bills—a splendid reproduction, almost defying detection. It is believed that the plates and presses from which they are made are right here in New York and the whole secret service force is at work trying to run the counterfeiters to earth. This is why our diamond case is going so slowly. They are so busy following up the counterfeiters they have no time for us."

Ray, much interested, leaned eagerly forward.

"A counterfeit ten dollar bill, did you say?" she demanded.

"Yes—it is a remarkable counterfeit. You would not know it from a good one. Only an expert can tell the difference. But all these crooks overreach themselves. Clever as they are, they usually leave some mark which betrays them. For example, in printing this bill which bears the head of Lincoln, they have spelled his first name 'Abrahem'—in other words, the engraver made an 'e' when it should have been 'a.'"

Ray jumped up, quite excited. Her eyes flashing, she cried.

"Isn't that strange! I have a new $10 bill, and I noticed to-day the queer spelling of Abraham. Wouldn't it be funny if I had one of the counterfeits?"

The lawyer smiled.

"It wouldn't be funny; it would be a tragedy, considering that in a short while from now I am to pay your bills. Where is the bank note?"

"I'll run up and get it. It's in my purse."

When she had disappeared, Steell turned to his hostess and said:

"Have you seen Signor Keralio lately?"

"Hardly—you know I dismissed him from the house."

The lawyer sat thoughtfully drumming his fingers on the table. Musingly, he said:

"Somehow I have a hunch that that fellow knows something about the diamonds. Does Kenneth ever see him?"

"I asked him the other day. He said he did not."

"That's strange!" exclaimed the lawyer. "It was only yesterday morning that I saw them together in a taxicab."

"Where?" demanded Helen, surprised.

"Away uptown. I had business up in the Bronx. I was driving my car and was near 200th street and going north when suddenly I had to steer to one side to allow a taxicab to pass. There were two men in it. I just chanced to glance inside and, to my surprise, I recognized your husband and Keralio."

"What time was that?"

"Very early—about nine o'clock."

"What direction?"

"They were coming south."

"Then he must have been with Keralio all night, for he didn't come home."

The lawyer was silent. Certainly here was a mystery which needed more detective talent than he possessed to clear up. Yet he would not rest until it was solved. To-morrow he would get Dick Reynolds busy, and they would go to work in earnest. The first thing to find out was what took Keralio and Kenneth to the Bronx.

"Does Keralio live in the Bronx?"

"I don't know," said Helen.

"I'll find out," said the lawyer, grimly.

At that moment Ray returned, holding out a new ten-dollar bill.

"I was right," she cried. "The name Abraham is spelled with an 'e.' Do you really think this is a counterfeit?"

The lawyer took the bill and examined it critically.

"I have no doubt of it," he answered. "There are other indications—the general appearance, the touch of the paper. Where did you get it?"

For a moment the young girl was puzzled.

"Let me think. Where did I get it. Oh yes, I know. Francois gave it to me."

"Francois!" exclaimed Helen.

The lawyer started and looked up in surprise.

"Francois, your brother-in-law's valet?"

"Yes—I wanted a $20 bill changed to pay for some things that came home from the store, and he went out and brought me some old bills and this new one."

The lawyer gave vent to a low, expressive whistle.

"Francois gave it to you, eh? Where is Francois?"

"I discharged him to-day for insolence," said Helen.

"He's gone!"

"Yes—he went shortly before you came in."

The lawyer jumped to his feet, a look of exultation on his face. Quickly, he said:

"Didn't you say that this Francois was formerly with Signor Keralio?"

"Yes—he was with him for years."

The lawyer gave a wild whoop of joy.

"Then we've got it—at last."

"Got what?" cried the women.

"A clue—a clue!" cried the lawyer, excitedly. "Can't you see it? Francois is hand in glove with Keralio—the master rogue who is making this counterfeit."

"What do you propose to do?"

"Find where Keralio lives—then, perhaps, we'll find the lost diamonds."

CHAPTER XVIII

"This way," whispered Dick, as he darted swiftly from door to door, "keep close behind me, and stick to the wall, or he'll see you."

But Francois was so utterly fagged after his long walk from the Elevated road, carrying his heavy suitcase, that he worried about nothing save his own discomfort. Unable to find a taxi, he had been compelled to tramp the entire distance, and the fatigue of it had made him peevish. He could have saved himself at least a mile if he had taken a more direct road, but Keralio's orders were explicit. He must always follow a circuitous route so as to throw possible pursuers off the scent. There was no disobeying the orders of the chief, so on he trudged, looking neither to right nor left, up one street, down another, now crossing an empty lot, now darting through a narrow alley, through the wastes and dreariness of Bronxville.

As he approached his journey's end, he accelerated his pace, going along so fast that it was as much as Dick and Steell could do to keep up with him. The night was dark and foggy, and at times they could not see him for the mist. But as he came within the glare of each lamp post, they could make out his lithe figure, scurrying along as if the devil himself were at his heels.

"Let's get up closer," gasped Dick, who was winded from the long chase. "I guess their den is in this neighborhood. He'll slip in somewhere and we'll lose him if we keep so far away."

"No—he may see us," whispered Steell cautiously. "We can make him out all right."

They increased their pace a little. The valet was less than two blocks away, and once he actually stopped and looked around as if to see if he was followed. Quickly Steell and Dick darted under a doorway, and, seeing nothing to arouse his suspicion, Francois went on.

The lawyer was taking no chances to-night. It was too good a game to spoil. That they were on the right trail at last he was morally certain. Ray's experience had given him the first clue. After that it was easy. For two days Dick had shadowed the valet, and seen him changing crisp $10 bills in half a dozen different places. The lawyer could have had him arrested at once, but he was after bigger game. It was not enough to arrest Francois. He was only the tool. They must get the man higher up, the man who employed him. That man, the lawyer felt equally confident, was Keralio. He was the master counter-feiter. The first step to take was to find out where the counter-feiting was done, where Keralio had his plant, and the only way to do this was to follow the valet to his master's secret den. For several days they had shadowed the Frenchman constantly, until to-night they were rewarded by seeing him start with a suit case in the direction of the Bronx. They quickly gave chase, the lawyer confident of results. It was not part of his plan, however, to hurry matters or do things prematurely. To-night they would merely reconnoiter. They would content themselves by watching the premises, seeing who came and went, and trying to obtain a glimpse of the interior. If the evidence was incriminating enough to make a raid successful, it would always be time enough to call in the police. Keralio, he was also well convinced, had something to do with the missing diamonds, and possibly the present investigation would throw some light on the mystery surrounding Kenneth himself. He had made no mention of his suspicions to Helen, but he could not help feeling that in some way, yet to be discovered, his old comrade had become involved with a band of crooks. How otherwise explain his acquaintance with Keralio, an utter stranger of dubious antecedents. How explain the loss of the diamonds? The explanation Kenneth had given was decidedly fishy. Parker did not believe a word of it—in fact, frankly expressed, his opinion was that his vice-president had disposed of the gems. Had he himself not seen Kenneth driving about the Bronx with Keralio at an impossible hour? Had not Helen discovered Francois conversing on intimate terms with his master? It all looked decidedly bad; only time could unravel it all. It was a fearful thing to suspect a man of Kenneth's standing, but everything pointed to his being involved in a vast network of crime.

He was aroused from his reflections by an exclamation of warning from his companion.

"Quick—there he goes!" whispered Dick.

The valet had suddenly made a sharp turn to the right, and was lost to view. But quick as he was, Dick was quicker. The young man was a little ahead of the lawyer, and, putting on a spurt of speed, he reached the corner just in time to see the Frenchman and suitcase disappear into a grimy, dilapidated looking tenement at the end of a blind alley.

"We've run the fox to earth," whispered Steell exultantly.

"Could any melodrama wish for a more appropriate *mise-en-scene*?" grinned Dick.

"Come opposite, and find out what we can see from the outside."

Crossing the street they took up positions in the shadow of a doorway.

The house which the Frenchman had entered was all dark and apparently tenantless, except on the top floor where lights could be faintly seen behind hermetically sealed shutters. Straining his ears, Steell thought he could hear the steady hum of machinery in motion. With an exclamation of satisfaction, he turned to his companion:

"We've got 'em, Dick, we've got 'em. Do you hear the presses going?"

The young man listened. The sound was plainly audible, but it was a muffled sound, as if the walls and windows were padded with mattresses to prevent any sounds of the operations within from reaching inquisitive, outside ears.

"Let's go upstairs," whispered Steell.

Recrossing the road, they entered the house and began to grope their way up the narrow, winding staircase. They could make only slow progress, not only because of the absence of light, but owing to the rotten condition of the stairs. Indescribably filthy and littered with all sorts of rubbish and broken glass, in some places the boards had broken through entirely, leaving gaping holes, which were so many dangerous pitfalls. Twice the lawyer came near breaking his neck.

At last they reached the top, both out of breath from the long and perilous climb.

"Hush—there it is!" whispered Dick pointing at the end of a narrow hall to a door from underneath which issued a faint glimmer of light.

Cautiously, noiselessly, treading on tiptoe, the lawyer and his companion crept along the passage until they came to the door. They listened. There was not a sound. Even the hum of machinery which they had heard in the street, had ceased. Could the inmates have taken alarm?

All at once they heard people talking. Instantly, Steell recognized the voice of Keralio. He was questioning someone, no doubt the valet. They listened.

"Well, did you carry out my orders?"

"*Oui*, monsieur, ze last of ze ten-dollar bills has been passed. I have ze money here."

"I did not mean that," broke in Keralio impatiently. "I mean as regards the child—"

"*Oui*, monsieur. Didn't you receive my telegram. I brought the child from Philadelphia yesterday evening."

Steell, puzzled, turned to his companion.

"What child are they talking about?" he whispered.

"I have no idea. Some more mischief they're up to, I guess."

Again Keralio's voice was heard asking:

"Where is Handsome to-day? I told him to come. Why isn't he here?"

"He's drinking again, monsieur. When he's drunk you can't do anything with him. He's getting ugly about ze diamonds."

Steell nudged his fellow eavesdropper.

"Did you hear that?" he whispered. "He spoke of diamonds!"

Keralio was heard bursting into a peal of savage laughter.

"Getting ugly is he? What does he want?"

"He says you promised him half of ze proceeds when ze diamonds were sold, and that now you are trying to do him out of it—He says he's sick of ze whole thing and will squeal to ze police unless you do ze right thing."

Straining every nerve to hear, Steell glued his ear to the door.

Keralio burst out fiercely:

"Squeal, will he, the dog? I'd like to know what will become of him when the final reckoning's paid. Will he tell the police that he was a drunken adventurer in the South African mining camps before his twin brother, Kenneth Traynor, arrived at Cape Town? Will he tell the police that he set the steamer afire, murdered his own brother, and, profiting by the extraordinary resemblance, returned to New York, passing himself off as the man who went away. No, he won't tell all that, will he? But I will. Did you bring the money? Let me see it."

The talking suddenly ceased, and was followed by a deep silence. Steell, staggered at this unexpected revelation, almost stumbled in his eagerness to hear more. Turning to his companion, he exclaimed in a horror-stricken whisper:

"My God! Did you hear that? It's even worse than I feared. They've done away with Kenneth. That man at the house is an impostor!"

"An impostor?" ejaculated Dick. "Impossible. Don't we all know Kenneth when we see him?"

"Nothing's impossible!" rejoined the lawyer hurriedly. "Kenneth had a twin brother—the resemblance was so extraordinary as children that no one knew them apart. The brother disappeared years ago. They thought him dead. Kenneth must have come across him in South Africa. This brother killed him and took his place. It's all clear to me now. We're in a den of assassins!"

Inside the conversation began again.

"Hush! Listen!" whispered Steell.

The voice of Keralio was once more raised in angry tones.

"Didn't I tell you that I wanted the child brought here

at once?"

"*Oui*, monsieur, but I could not. I had ze rest of ze money to get rid of and ze suitcase to carry. I will bring her in a taxi to-morrow."

"Where is she?"

"Safe in the care of the woman who runs my boarding house."

"When did you bring her from Philadelphia?"

"Yesterday afternoon."

"Did you have any trouble?"

"*Non*, monsieur. I didn't even have to go to ze house, although I had a plausible story all ready. I was going to say that Mrs. Traynor had sent me to fetch Miss Dorothy because her mother wanted her home for ze coming marriage of Miss Ray. But it wasn't necessary to lie about it. I found ze child playing in ze street near the house. I merely told her her mamma wanted her to come home, gave her some candy, and she followed me willingly enough."

"By this time the alarm has been given."

"Monsieur. They probably telegraphed Mrs. Traynor last night that ze child was missing—"

The voices again stopped. Steell, his face white, and fists clenched, turned to his companion:

"Good Heavens, Dick, did you hear that? They've kidnapped Mrs. Traynor's little girl—no doubt, with the idea of demanding ransom. Thank God, we're in time to frustrate that crime—"

"Hush!" exclaimed his companion. "Listen!"

Keralio proceeded:

"Now you understand what you are to do. You bring the child here to-morrow morning. Meantime, I have already written in a disguised hand to Mrs. Traynor telling her that her child is safe—for the present, and that if she wants to see her she must come here to-morrow afternoon. I warned her that if she communicated with the police or informed any of her friends, the child would be put to death before it would be possible to effect a rescue. That ought to bring her here—"

"Would monsieur go as far as to kill—"

"Why not," demanded Keralio fiercely. "I permit nothing to stand in the way of my will. That woman can save her child's life, but she must pay the price I ask. She shall learn what it costs to dismiss me from her house—"

The valet was heard to chuckle as he said:

"I don't love her any too much myself. She discharged me from her employ the other day so haughtily I felt like a whipped cur."

Again there was silence, followed by a muffled hammering.

"They're taking the printing press apart," whispered Dick, who through the keyhole, had managed to get a glimpse of machinery. "If we don't act quickly, they'll get away with all the evidence. Hadn't we better go and call the police?"

For answer, the lawyer put his fingers to his lips with a warning gesture, and beckoning the young man to follow, retraced his steps on tiptoe along the narrow, dark hall and down the filthy, winding staircase. Not a word was spoken by either man until they reached the street. Once in the open air, the lawyer turned and said:

Arthur Hornblow

"Dick, we've uncovered as black a plot as was ever hatched in hell. If we don't queer the game and put them all in the chair it won't be my fault. We can't bring poor Kenneth back to life, but we can and will revenge his cowardly murder. It will be a positive joy to me to see that arch-scoundrel Keralio electrocuted."

"What do you propose to do?" asked his companion. "Hadn't we better call Mrs. Traynor on the telephone and warn her before it's too late?"

The lawyer was silent for a few moments. Then meditatively, he said:

"No, that would be a mistake. No doubt, by this time, she has received Keralio's anonymous letter. She is probably frantic with anxiety over the news of her child's disappearance, and will respond eagerly to any clue that promises to take her to her child. If we warned her she would pay no heed. She might pretend to, but only to pacify us. Afraid that punishment might be visited on the child, she would obey the warning not to talk, and she will come here to Keralio's flat to-morrow at the time the letter stated. Of course, she has no idea Keralio wrote the letter. But even if she had, it would make no difference. I know her. She would run any risk to save her child."

"I think you're right," replied Dick, "but how, then, will you help her? There is no knowing what Keralio's object is in enticing her here—you can be sure it's nothing good."

"Precisely—that's why we, too, must be on hand, together with a strong force of detectives. We'll get them all. There will be no possible escape. We'll surround the house with men. They'll be caught like rats in a trap."

The lawyer turned to go.

"Where are you bound now?" asked Dick.

"To police headquarters!"

Arthur Hornblow

CHAPTER XIX

"There—take a little water—you're much better now!" said the nurse, soothingly.

The patient swallowed greedily the cooling drink handed to him, and, tired even by that small effort, fell back on his pillows exhausted.

"Where am I?" he inquired of the comely young woman, who in neat service uniform, hovered about the bed.

"You're in St. Mary's Hospital."

"In New York?" he queried.

"No—San Francisco—"

He was too weak to question further, but his hollow blue eyes followed her as she moved here and there, attending skilfully and swiftly to the duties of the sick room. Presently he made another venture:

"Have I been ill long?"

"Yes—very long."

"What's the matter?"

"Concussion of the brain, pneumonia and shock. You are

much better now, but you mustn't talk so much or you may have a relapse."

He asked no more, but passed his hand over his brow in a bewildered sort of way. Presently, he began again:

"Does my wife come to see me?"

The nurse stopped in her work and looked at him curiously. In surprise, she exclaimed:

"Your wife! Have you a wife?"

It was his turn now to be surprised. In somewhat peevish tone he said:

"Of course I've a wife—everyone knows that."

"What's her name?"

"Helen—Helen Traynor." Enthusiastically, he added: "Oh, you'd just love my wife if you only knew her. She's the sweetest, the most unselfish—"

The nurse looked at him curiously.

"So your name is Traynor, is it? We've tried to find out for a long time. But there were no marks on your clothes when you were picked up. We did not know who you were and so have not been able to communicate with any of your friends. We guessed you were a man of social position by your hands and teeth, and we knew your name began with a T because of the monogram on the signet ring on your finger."

"Pick me up?" he echoed. "Where did they pick me up? What has happened? Was it an accident?"

"You were found unconscious, drifting in the ocean, clinging to a spar, and were brought here by a sailing vessel. You had a fracture of the skull and you were half drowned. It is supposed that you were one of the passengers of the *Abyssinia*, which took fire and went down two days after leaving Cape Town, but as several passengers and officers whose bodies were never found also had names beginning with T, it was impossible to identify you."

As he listened, the vacant, stupid expression on his face gradually gave place to a more alert, intelligent look. Indistinctly, vaguely, he recalled things that had happened. Slowly his brain cells began to work.

He remembered cabling to Helen from Cape Town telling her of his sailing on the *Abyssinia*. He recalled the incidents of the first day at sea. The weather was beautiful. Everything pointed to a good voyage. Who was traveling with him? He could not remember. Oh, yes, now he knew. Francois, his valet, and that other queer fellow he had picked up at the diamond mines—his twin brother. Yes, it all came back to him now.

Why had he gone to the diamond mines? Yes, now he knew—to take back to New York the two big stones found on the Company's land. He had them safe in a belt he wore round his waist next to his skin. The second night out he went to bed about midnight and was fast asleep when suddenly he heard shouts of "Fire! Fire!" Jumping up and looking out of his cabin he saw stewards and passengers running excitedly about. There was a reddish glare and a suffocating smell of smoke. Quickly he buckled on the belt with the diamonds, and, slipping on his trousers, went out. The electric lights had gone out. The ship was in complete darkness. From all sides came shouts of men and screams of frightened women. It was a scene of utter demoralization and horror. He was groping his way along the narrow passage, when, suddenly, out of the gloom a man sprang upon him, and, taken entirely by surprise, he was borne to the deck before he had time to defend himself. He could not see the man's face and thought it was one of the passengers or sailors who had gone mad, but when he felt a tug at his belt where the diamonds were, he knew he had to do with a thief.

He fought back with all his strength, but he was unarmed, while the stranger had a black jack which he used unmercifully, raining fearful blows on his head. The struggle was too unequal to last. Weak from loss of blood, he relaxed his grip, and the thief, dealing one fearful parting blow, tore away the belt and disappeared. His life blood was flowing away, he felt sick and dizzy, but just as the thief turned to run he managed to get a glimpse of his face. Now he remembered that face—it was the face of his twin brother—the man he had rescued from starvation on the *veldt*.

Yes, it all came back to him now, like a horrible nightmare. What had happened since then? How could he tell, since all this time his mind had been a blank? Helen, no doubt, believed him dead. Mr. Parker and all the others thought he had gone down with the ship. But what of his valet, Francois, and his cowardly, murderous brother—were they saved? If so, the thief had the diamonds, and had probably disposed of them by this time. Perhaps there might still be time to capture the would-be assassin and save the gems for the Americo-African Company. Brother or no brother, he would have no more pity on the unnatural, miserable cutthroat. The first step was to let his friends know where he was. He must telegraph at once to Helen.

Yet, on second thought, it would not be wise to do that. If Helen really believed him dead and was now mourning his loss, it might be almost a fatal shock if suddenly she were to receive a telegram saying he was alive. Such shocks have been known to kill people. A better plan would be to get well as soon as possible, leave the hospital, and go to New York. Once there, he could go quietly to his office and learn how matters were.

The days passed, the convalescent making speedy progress toward recovery, and in a few weeks more he was able to leave the hospital. Making himself known quietly to a San Francisco business acquaintance, he was quickly supplied with funds and immediately he turned his face homeward.

The long, overland journey was tedious and exhausting, especially in his present weakened condition, and even those who knew him well would hardly have recognized in the pale emaciated looking stranger with ill fitting clothes and untrimmed full growth of beard who emerged from the train at the Grand Central Station, the carefully dressed, well groomed Kenneth Traynor who, only a few months before, had sailed away from New York on the *Mauretania*.

The noise and turmoil of the big metropolis, in striking contrast to the quiet and seclusion of the sick room in which he had lived for so many weeks, astonished him. The crowds of suburbanites rushing frantically for trains, elbowing and pushing in their anxiety to get home, the strident hoarse cries of newsboys, the warning shouts of wagon drivers as they drove recklessly here and there at murderous speed, the blowing of auto horns, the ceaseless hum and roar of the big city's heavy traffic—all this bewildered and dazed him. At first he did not remember just in what direction to turn, whether he lived in the East or West side, uptown or down. But as he got more accustomed to his surroundings, it all came back to him. How stupid—of course he had to go downtown to 20th Street. Once more he was himself again. Hailing a taxi, he started for Gramercy Park.

Conflicting emotions stirred his breast as he drew near his home. What joy it would be to clasp Helen once more in his arms. How delighted she would be to see him! Then he was filled with anxiety, a sudden feeling of dread came over him. Suppose some misfortune, some calamity had happened during his absence! Helen might have met with some accident. Baby might have been ill. The worst might have happened. He would never have heard. Perhaps he was only going home to find his happiness wrecked forever.

The driver made his way with difficulty down Fifth Avenue, threading his way in and out the entanglement of carriages and automobiles, until, after a ten minutes' run, turned into Gramercy Park and pulled up short on the curb of the

Traynor residence.

Eagerly Kenneth put his head out of the window and scanned the windows for a glimpse of the loved one, but no one, not even a servant, was visible. The house looked deserted. His misgivings returned. Stepping out hastily, he paid the driver, and, running up the steps, rang the bell.

Roberts, the faithful old butler, who had been in the family service for years, came to open. Seeing a rather shabbily attired person outside, he held the door partly closed and demanded, suspiciously:

"Who is it you wish to see?"

Irritated at the manner of his reception, Kenneth gave the door a push that nearly knocked the servant over. Angrily, he exclaimed:

"What's the matter, Roberts? Didn't you see it was me?"

The butler, who had recovered himself, and now believed he had to do with a crank or some person under the influence of liquor, again barred the way. Trying to push the unwelcome visitor out, he said soothingly:

"Come now, my good man, you've made a mistake. You don't live here."

Struck almost speechless with amazement at the brazen impudence of one whom he had always regarded as a model servant, Kenneth turned round as if about to make a wrathful outburst. As he turned, the light from the open door fell full on his face and now for the first time Roberts saw the visitor's features. With a startled exclamation the man fell backward. For a moment he was so surprised that he could not speak. Then, in an awe-stricken whisper, he cried:

"Who are you?"

For a moment Kenneth thought the man had suddenly become insane. For his own servant not to know him was too ridiculous. At that moment he caught a glimpse of himself in the mirror of the hat stand. Ah, now he understood. The beard and emaciated face had made quite a difference—no wonder the man failed to recognize him. Breaking into laughter he exclaimed:

"No wonder you didn't recognize me, Roberts. I have changed a little, haven't I? I've grown a beard since I saw you last and been through a regular mill. But you know me now don't you—I'm your long lost master."

The servant shook his head. Still closely scrutinizing Kenneth's face as if greatly puzzled, he said:

"You're not my master, sir. Mr. Kenneth Traynor left the house some ten minutes before you arrived."

Kenneth stared at the man as if he thought he had gone clean out of his mind.

"I went out ten minutes before I arrived," he echoed. "What kind of nonsense is that, Roberts?"

"I didn't say *you* went out," replied the servant, beginning to lose his patience. "I said Mr. Kenneth Traynor went out. You are not Mr. Kenneth Traynor."

"Then who in the name of heaven am I?"

"I haven't the remotest idea," retorted the man. Condescendingly, he went on: "I admit you look a little like the master." Impatiently he added:

"You must excuse me. I want to close the door."

Instead of obeying the hint to withdraw, Kenneth strode further into the house, the protesting and indignant butler at his heels.

"You must really go," said the servant.

Kenneth turned around.

"Roberts—don't be a fool. Don't you know me? I know why you don't recognize me. You all think me dead, but I'm very much alive. I did not go down on the *Abyssinia*. I was picked up and taken to San Francisco and have been in a hospital there ever since. I have just come home. Where's my wife?"

The butler stared and stood motionless, as if not knowing what to make of it.

"But you came home long ago."

"Who came home?"

"You did."

"No, I didn't. I've been in San Francisco all the time. How could I be here if I was sick in a San Francisco hospital?"

"Then who is the other Mr. Traynor?"

Now it was Kenneth's turn to be surprised.

"The other Mr. Traynor?" he echoed stupefied.

"Yes—the gentleman who looks more like you than you do yourself. He arrived here a month ago. We all took him for you."

For the first time a light broke in on the darkness. Who was the person who looked so like him that he could successfully impersonate him? Who could it be but the man who left him for dead on the *Abyssinia* after murderously assaulting him? Suddenly a horrible thought came to him. Grasping the butler's arm he exclaimed:

"My wife? Is she well?"

"Yes, sir. Mrs. Traynor's quite well."

"And Dorothy?"

"Quite well, sir."

"Thank God!"

The servant hesitated.

"That is—sir—Miss Dorothy—"

"Out with it, man. Out with it."

"Mrs. Traynor's being greatly worried sir, lately. Miss Dorothy was at her aunt's in Philadelphia—"

"Yes, yes—"

"Someone's run away with Miss Dorothy. She's been kidnapped."

"My God!"

"But Mrs. Traynor has a clue. She got a letter yesterday, saying where the child was. She wouldn't confide in any of us and she left here only half an hour ago to go to the place."

Again Kenneth was seized by panic.

"Gone to a kidnapper's den. Great God! She's running a terrible risk. Where has she gone? I'll go to her."

"I don't know, sir, but Mr. Steell may know—"

"Ah, that's right. I'll go and see Steell."

Not waiting to say more he rushed down the steps, and, hailing another taxi, went off at full speed in the direction of Wilbur Steell's office.

CHAPTER XX

The startling news from Philadelphia that Dorothy had suddenly disappeared and was believed to have been kidnapped, fell upon the Traynor home with the crushing force of a bombshell. At first Helen refused to credit the report. It seemed impossible that any new suffering was to be inflicted upon her after what she had already endured. White faced, her whole being shaken by emotion, she read and re-read her aunt's letter, telling of the child's mysterious disappearance, and when at last she could read it no more because of the tears that blinded her, she threw herself limp and broken hearted into Ray's arms. Hysterically she cried:

"What have I done that I should be made to suffer in this way? My God! Where is my child? This maddening suspense will kill me."

Ray tried to soothe her. Reassuringly, she said:

"Don't worry, dear. Everything will be all right. A general alarm has been sent out. The police all over the country are searching high and low. It's only a question of a few hours and you'll have good news."

But the hours passed and no news came to cheer the distracted, broken-hearted mother. Dorothy had disappeared completely, leaving no trace, no clue behind.

There was neither rest nor peace for the Traynor household

that day. Helen, almost out of her mind from grief and worry, refused to eat or sleep until news of the missing child was received. In her agony she went down on her knees and prayed as she had never prayed before that her child be restored to her.

Her little daughter was, she felt, the one link that still bound her to life. To her husband she felt she could not turn for sympathy. The romance of their early married life had been shattered forever by the extraordinary change that had come over him. He had long since ceased to be to her any more than a name. In her heart, she had come to despise and detest him as much as before she had worshiped the very ground he trod. It was an astonishing revulsion of feeling which she was powerless to explain; she only knew that the old love, the old passion he had awakened was now quite dead. He inspired in her no more affection or feeling than the merest stranger. Ever since his return from South Africa they had lived apart. Ever since that first night of his return when their tete-a-tete in the library was interrupted by the bogus telegram, he had quite ceased his amorous advances. He seemed anxious to avoid her. Only on rare occasions, and then it was by accident, did they find themselves in each other's company.

In fact, he was practically never home, living almost exclusively at the club, where he went the pace with associates of his choosing, mostly gamblers and men about town. He had begun to drink hard and when not in pool rooms or at the races, betting recklessly on the horses, squandering such huge sums, and overdrawing his check account so often that the bank was compelled to ask him to desist, he sat in the barrooms with his cronies till all hours of the morning when he would be brought home in a condition of shocking intoxication. Happily Helen was spared the spectacle of the degradation of a man she once had loved with all the force of her virgin soul. Roberts, the butler, aided by the other servants, smuggled their intoxicated master up to his room, where he remained until sober, when he went back to his club only to repeat the same performance.

To such a man she could not turn for aid or consolation in the hour of this new misfortune. Indeed, ever since his return, he had been strangely indifferent to the welfare of the child, never asking after her or expressing a desire to see her. At times it seemed as if he had forgotten that he had a child. By some strange metamorphosis he had developed into an unnatural father as well as a brutal, indifferent husband.

But to Helen, alone save for the devoted companionship of her sister, this was anxiety and suffering enough. Only twenty-four hours had passed since the child disappeared, but to the unhappy mother it seemed as many years. Constantly at the telephone, expecting each moment to hear that the police had been successful in finding the child, she was gradually wearing herself away to a shadow. Breakfast she left untouched. Lunch she refused to eat. In vain Ray remonstrated with her. If she went on like that she would fall ill. But still Helen refused. Tears choked her, and morning wore into afternoon and still no news.

After lunch Ray went out to see if Mr. Steell could help them, promising to return as soon as possible. Helen sat and waited alone. The clock was just striking two o'clock when the front doorbell rang and a letter was brought to her. She did not recognize the writing, but eagerly she tore it open. Instinctively, she felt it concerned her missing darling. The letter read as follows:

No. — Lasalle Street, Bronx. Friday.

Madame:

Your child is safe and in good hands. She wants to see her mother. If you come this afternoon (Friday) to the above address you can see her. It is the house with the closed green shutters. But if you value your child's life you must come unaccompanied, and you must inform no one of the contents of this letter, not even the members of your family. If you disobey, swift punishment will follow and your child will suffer. Climb eight flights and knock three times on door at end of passage.—X.

There was no signature. The person who wrote it evidently had reasons of his own for wishing to remain concealed. That money would be demanded was more than probable. What other motive could the kidnapper have? Money she would give—all she had in the world, if only she could get back her precious child. That a visit to such a place unattended was full of danger she did not stop to consider. She only knew that her child was close by—here in New York—and had asked for her. Not for a moment did she listen to the warnings of prudence. Go she must, and immediately. She did not even stop to leave a note of explanation for Ray. Stuffing some money in a bag, she left the house, saying she would return soon.

Taking the Third Avenue "L" she left the train at Tremont Avenue, and, after considerable difficulty, found the house indicated in the letter. Yes, there were the closed green shutters. At first, on seeing it apparently untenanted, she thought she must have made a mistake in the number, but, finding that there was no other place near by that answered the description as well, she decided to risk climbing the long flight of stairs.

Arrived on the top floor, breathless from the unusual exertion, she saw a long narrow passage, and, at the end of that, a door. That, no doubt, was the place. Her heart beating violently, she went up to the door and gave the three knocks. For a moment or so there was no answer. A profound stillness reigned. Then she heard footsteps approaching, The next instant, the door was thrown open and a man's voice, which sounded somewhat familiar, told her to enter.

At first when she went in, she could see nothing. All the shutters of the windows looking on the street were closed, and the only light was that which filtered through the slats. It was an ordinary, cheap flat, with no carpets on the floors and little or no furniture. On the floor, scattered here and there, were nailed-up boxes, and parts of machinery, some already crated, as if to be taken away.

"So you've come! I thought you would," said a voice behind her.

She turned and found herself face to face with Signor Keralio.

At first she was so astonished that she was speechless. Then her instinct prompted her to turn and flee. If this man had caused her to be decoyed to this house it could be for no good purpose. But there was no way of egress. The front door was closed and locked. Not a human soul was within call. She was alone in an empty house with the one man she distrusted and feared more than any one else in the world.

Making an effort to conceal her alarm, she turned and faced him boldly:

"What are you doing here?" she asked.

He smiled—a horrid, cynical smile she knew only too well.

"Has not a man the right to be in his own home?"

She started back in surprise.

"This your home?" she exclaimed, glancing around at the scanty and shabby furnishings.

He shrugged his shoulders.

"Oh, don't judge by appearances. I'm really very comfortable here. It's away from the world. I like to work undisturbed." Significantly, he added: "Then, you see, it is all my own. I am quite at home here in my own house. No one can put me out—not even you—"

She raised her hand deprecatingly.

"Please don't remind me of that. I have forgotten it long ago."

His eyes flashed dangerously as he made a step near and exclaimed:

"You have, but I have not. I have not forgotten that you put me out of your house ignominiously as one turns out a servant. I have neither forgotten nor forgiven. That is why you are here to-day."

She looked at him in utter astonishment.

"What do you mean?"

He bowed and, with mock courtesy, waved her to a seat.

"I will tell you. Did you receive a letter to-day?"

"Yes—I did."

"You came here in answer to that letter."

"Yes—I did."

"Do you know who wrote that letter?"

"No—not the least."

"It was I—I wrote the letter."

With a stifled cry of mingled fright and amazement, Helen jumped up from the chair.

"You wrote the letter?" she exclaimed, incredulously.

He nodded.

"Yes—I wrote the letter."

Her eyes opened wide with terror, her hands clasped together nervously, she exclaimed:

"Then you are—"

He bowed.

"Exactly. I am the kidnapper of your child—"

Speechless, she stared at him, her large black eyes opened wide with terror. Looking wildly about her as if seeking her little daughter, she gasped:

"Dorothy? Dorothy here? Where is she?"

"She is safe," he replied calmly.

"Where is she, where is she? Take me to her!" she cried, distractedly, going up to him and clasping her hands in humble supplication.

He shook off the hand which, in her maternal anxiety, she had laid on his arm. Lighting a cigarette, he gave a low laugh.

"Plenty of time. There's no hurry. You're not going yet."

Anxiously, she scrutinized his face, as if trying to read his meaning.

"She's going when I go, isn't she?"

He shrugged his shoulders.

"That depends—on you."

"What do you mean?"

Again he waved her to a seat.

"Sit down and I'll tell you."

Trembling, she dropped once more on to a chair and waited. He puffed deliberately at his cigarette for a few moments and then, turning his glance in her direction, he smiled in a peculiar, horrible way and his eyes ran over her figure in a way that made the crimson rush furiously to her cheek. There was no mistaking that smile. It was the bold, lustful look of the voluptuary who enjoys letting his eyes feast on the prey that he knows cannot now escape him.

"Mrs. Traynor," he began in the caressing, dulcet tones which she feared more than his anger, "you are an exceptional woman. To most men of my temperament you would not appeal. They would find your beauty too statuesque and cold. I know you are clever, but love cannot feed on intellect alone, I have loved many women, but never a woman just like you. Your coldness, your haughty reserve, your refinement would intimidate most men and keep them at a distance, but not me. Your aloofness, your indifference only spurs me, only adds to the acuteness of my desire. I swore to myself that I would conquer you, overcome your resistance, bend you to my will. You turned me out of your home.

I swore to be avenged."

He stopped for a moment and watched her closely as if studying and enjoying the effect of his words. Then, amid a cloud of blue tobacco smoke, he went on:

"I knew only one way to win you—it was to humiliate you, to place you in a position where you would have to come to me on your knees."

She half rose from her chair.

"I would never do that," she cried. "I would rather die!"

"Oh, yes, you will," he continued, calmly, making a gesture to

Arthur Hornblow

her to remain seated. "When I've told you all, you'll see things in a different light." Fixing her steadily with his piercing black eyes, he asked: "Have you noticed any difference in your husband since his return."

She looked up quickly.

"Yes—what does it mean? Can you explain?"

He nodded.

"Did you ever hear your husband speak of a twin brother he once had?"

Her face turned white as death and her heart throbbing violently, she stared helplessly at her persecutor. She tried to be calm, but she could not. Yet, why be so alarmed, why should this single question so agitate her? In the deepest recesses of her being she knew that it was her unerring instinct warning her that she was about to hear something that would entail worse suffering than any she had yet endured.

"Yes—yes—why do you ask?" she gasped.

"You all thought the brother dead."

"Yes."

"You were mistaken. He is alive."

"Where is he?" she faltered.

"Here in New York."

"Where?"

"In your house. The man who returned home was not your husband. He was your husband's twin brother."

She looked at him as one bewildered, as if she did not understand what he was saying, as if words had suddenly lost their meaning. Her face, white as in death, she faltered:

"Not Kenneth—then where is Kenneth?"

"He is dead!"

Her powers of speech paralyzed, her large eyes starting from their sockets from terror, an expression of mute helpless agony on her beautiful face, she looked up at him with horror. Not yet could she fully grasp the meaning of his words. At last the frightful spell was broken. With an effort the words came:

"Then you," she cried. "You are his assassin!"

He shook his head as he replied carelessly:

"No—not I—his brother!"

She gave a cry of anguish and, starting to her feet, made a movement forward, her hands clutching convulsively at her throat. Air! air! She must have air. She felt sick and dizzy. The room was spinning round like a top, and then everything grew dark. Lurching heavily forward she would have fallen had he not caught her.

Instantly she shrank from the contact as from something unclean, and with a low moan sank down on a chair and buried her face in her hands. Her instinct had told her true. Her loved one was dead, she would never see him again, and that man who had come into the sanctity of her home and fondled her in his arms was his murderer. Oh, it was too horrible!

The bitter, cynical smile was still on Keralio's lips as he went on:

"You see the folly of resisting me. Had you surrendered at that time all might have been well. The price was not too much to pay. I would have been discreet. No one but ourselves would have known that you and I were—"

He did not complete the sentence, for at that moment she sprang forward like an enraged tiger cat, and, seizing a cane that stood close by, struck him across the face with all the force of her outraged womanhood.

"Murderer! Assassin!" she cried indignantly. "How dare you talk like that to me? I will denounce you to the whole world. I will not rest till I see you and that other scoundrel punished and my poor husband is avenged. On leaving here I shall go direct to the police."

Imbued with strength she never dreamed she possessed, she was about to hit him again when he seized the cane and threw it away. But across his pale, handsome face lay a telltale red mark, the smart of which burned into his soul.

His eyes flashed with anger and he made a visible effort to control himself. He took a step forward and, as he advanced she saw an expression in his face which prompted her to retreat precipitately. It was a dangerous look, the look of a man who knew he had a helpless woman in his power, a man who was desperate and would stop at nothing to encompass his ends. Now thoroughly frightened, she looked around for some way to escape. The windows were impossible, the only way was by the door and he barred the way. Besides, she would never go without her child.

He noticed the movement and look of alarm, and he smiled. Continuing to advance, he said:

"There's no use making a fuss. No one could hear you if you shouted for help till the crack of doom. You are alone with me—and absolutely in my power. Do as I ask and there is nothing you shall not have. Refuse, and I answer for nothing. Come—"

Her whole body trembling, her face white with terror, she kept on retreating:

"Leave me alone!" she gasped, "or I will scream."

"Scream away," he laughed. "There's no one here to hear you."

Suddenly he made a quick lunge forward and seized her. She struggled and resisted with all the energy born of despair, pushing, twisting, scratching. But they were too unevenly matched. She was like an infant in the grasp of an Hercules. Slowly, she felt her strength leaving her. His iron grasp gradually closed on her, nearer and nearer he drew her into his embrace.

With a last, superhuman effort, she managed to wrench herself free, out of his grip, and breaking completely away, she fled into the next room. But he was after her in a minute and again seized her, but not before she screamed at the top of her voice:

"Help! Help! Kenneth! Wilbur! Help! Help!"

He tried to gag her mouth to stifle her cries, but it was too late. His quick ear caught the sound of approaching footsteps in the outside hall. Almost at the same instant there was a loud knocking at the door.

Keralio fell back, his face white and tense. Had his plans failed at the eleventh hour, could anyone have played him false? If the game was up, they should never take him alive. Leaving Helen, he drew a revolver, and, going quickly into the inner hall, he waited in grim silence for the visitors to force an entrance.

"Open the door, or we'll break it in!" shouted a stern voice outside. "There's no use resisting. The place is surrounded."

Still no answer. Keralio stood grimly in the shadow of the parlor doorway, revolver in hand, while Helen cowered in the

Arthur Hornblow

inner room, in momentary expectation of a tragedy.

Crash! The front door fell in, shattered into a thousand splinters, and through the breach thus made rushed Wilbur Steell, Dick Reynolds, and half a score husky Central Office detectives, revolvers in hand.

"There is he!" cried the lawyer, pointing to Keralio.

Quick as a flash, the Italian raised the revolver and fired, the bullet entering the plastered wall an inch away from the lawyer's head. Almost simultaneously, another pistol shot rang out, but this time the aim was truer, for, with a cry of baffled rage, Keralio threw his arms above his head and fell to the floor dead. Quickly, one of the detectives stooped down and compared his face with a photograph he had taken from his pocket.

"Yes—" he exclaimed; "that's the fellow—well known counterfeiter. Did time in San Quentin and Joliet. Known as Baron Rapp, Richard Barton and a dozen other aliases. He's one of the slickest rogues in the country. We've got the valet safe downstairs. I guess he'll get twenty years."

But Steell had not waited to hear about Keralio. There were others more important to think about. Rushing into the inner room, he found Helen prostrate, half fainting from fright.

"Thank God, I'm in time!" he exclaimed.

"Dorothy," she murmured weakly. "Save Dorothy! She's somewhere here."

Going into another room, the lawyer found the little girl fast asleep on a bed. Bringing her to her mother, he said tenderly:

"Here's your treasure. Now you can be happy."

She shook her head. The nightmare of what Keralio had told

her, still obsessed her.

"No—" she shuddered; "—never again. They have killed him!"

To her surprise, the lawyer, instead of sharing her sorrow, actually smiled.

"Helen," he said; "I have a great surprise for you. A friend has accompanied me here. He called at your house to-day, but you had just left, so he called on me. You have not seen him since he sailed away three months ago on the *Mauretania*."

She listened bewildered. Her color came and went. What did he mean? Could it be possible that—no, had not Keralio said he was dead? Trembling with suppressed emotion, she whispered:

"Tell me—what is it—tell me—"

For all reply, the lawyer went to the door and beckoned to someone who had waited in the outer hall. A moment later a man entered, a tall, well set figure that was strangely familiar. Straining her eyes through her tears, it seemed to her that her mind must be playing her some trick, for there before her, stood Kenneth, not the impostor her instinct had warned her to detest and avoid, but the real Kenneth she had loved, the father of her child. With a joyous exclamation, she tottered forward.

"Kenneth!" she cried.

The man, his athletic form broken by sobs, opened his arms.

"My own precious darling!"

A moment later they were clasped in each other's arms. Ah, now she knew that he had come home! This, indeed, was the husband she loved. There was no deception this time. Wonderingly, she turned to Steell.

"How did it happen?" she asked wonderingly.

"We'll tell you later—not now," he replied.

She shuddered as she asked in a low voice.

"But where is his brother?"

"Dead! He shot himself at the club. Kenneth and I went to confront him at the club before coming here. It was his only way out."

The detective stepped forward. Addressing the lawyer and holding out two enormous diamonds that sparkled like fire in the sunlight, he said:

"We've just found these, together with a lot of counterfeit money."

The lawyer laughed as he took charge of the diamonds.

"It'll please Mr. Parker to see these. Come, Dick. Our work is done."

Kenneth put his arms around his wife.

"Safe in port at last, dear."

"You'll never go away again," she murmured through her tears.

Choose from Thousands of 1stWorldLibrary Classics By

A. M. Barnard
Ada Leverson
Adolphus William Ward
Aesop
Agatha Christie
Alexander Aaronsohn
Alexander Kielland
Alexandre Dumas
Alfred Gatty
Alfred Ollivant
Alice Duer Miller
Alice Turner Curtis
Alice Dunbar
Allen Chapman
Alleyne Ireland
Ambrose Bierce
Amelia E. Barr
Amory H. Bradford
Andrew Lang
Andrew McFarland Davis
Andy Adams
Angela Brazil
Anna Alice Chapin
Anna Sewell
Annie Besant
Annie Hamilton Donnell
Annie Payson Call
Annie Roe Carr
Annonaymous
Anton Chekhov
Archibald Lee Fletcher
Arnold Bennett
Arthur C. Benson
Arthur Conan Doyle
Arthur M. Winfield
Arthur Ransome
Arthur Schnitzler
Arthur Train
Atticus
B.H. Baden-Powell
B. M. Bower
B. C. Chatterjee
Baroness Emmuska Orczy
Baroness Orczy
Basil King
Bayard Taylor
Ben Macomber
Bertha Muzzy Bower
Bjornstjerne Bjornson

Booth Tarkington
Boyd Cable
Bram Stoker
C. Collodi
C. E. Orr
C. M. Ingleby
Carolyn Wells
Catherine Parr Traill
Charles A. Eastman
Charles Amory Beach
Charles Dickens
Charles Dudley Warner
Charles Farrar Browne
Charles Ives
Charles Kingsley
Charles Klein
Charles Hanson Towne
Charles Lathrop Pack
Charles Romyn Dake
Charles Whibley
Charles Willing Beale
Charlotte M. Braeme
Charlotte M. Yonge
Charlotte Perkins Stetson
Clair W. Hayes
Clarence Day Jr.
Clarence E. Mulford
Clemence Housman
Confucius
Coningsby Dawson
Cornelis DeWitt Wilcox
Cyril Burleigh
D. H. Lawrence
Daniel Defoe
David Garnett
Dinah Craik
Don Carlos Janes
Donald Keyhoe
Dorothy Kilner
Dougan Clark
Douglas Fairbanks
E. Nesbit
E. P. Roe
E. Phillips Oppenheim
E. S. Brooks
Earl Barnes
Edgar Rice Burroughs
Edith Van Dyne
Edith Wharton

Edward Everett Hale
Edward J. O'Biren
Edward S. Ellis
Edwin L. Arnold
Eleanor Atkins
Eleanor Hallowell Abbott
Eliot Gregory
Elizabeth Gaskell
Elizabeth McCracken
Elizabeth Von Arnim
Ellem Key
Emerson Hough
Emilie F. Carlen
Emily Bronte
Emily Dickinson
Enid Bagnold
Enilor Macartney Lane
Erasmus W. Jones
Ernie Howard Pie
Ethel May Dell
Ethel Turner
Ethel Watts Mumford
Eugene Sue
Eugenie Foa
Eugene Wood
Eustace Hale Ball
Evelyn Everett-green
Everard Cotes
F. H. Cheley
F. J. Cross
F. Marion Crawford
Fannie E. Newberry
Federick Austin Ogg
Ferdinand Ossendowski
Fergus Hume
Florence A. Kilpatrick
Fremont B. Deering
Francis Bacon
Francis Darwin
Frances Hodgson Burnett
Frances Parkinson Keyes
Frank Gee Patchin
Frank Harris
Frank Jewett Mather
Frank L. Packard
Frank V. Webster
Frederic Stewart Isham
Frederick Trevor Hill
Frederick Winslow Taylor

Friedrich Kerst
Friedrich Nietzsche
Fyodor Dostoyevsky
G.A. Henty
G.K. Chesterton
Gabrielle E. Jackson
Garrett P. Serviss
Gaston Leroux
George A. Warren
George Ade
Geroge Bernard Shaw
George Cary Eggleston
George Durston
George Ebers
George Eliot
George Gissing
George MacDonald
George Meredith
George Orwell
George Sylvester Viereck
George Tucker
George W. Cable
George Wharton James
Gertrude Atherton
Gordon Casserly
Grace E. King
Grace Gallatin
Grace Greenwood
Grant Allen
Guillermo A. Sherwell
Gulielma Zollinger
Gustav Flaubert
H. A. Cody
H. B. Irving
H.C. Bailey
H. G. Wells
H. H. Munro
H. Irving Hancock
H. R. Naylor
H. Rider Haggard
H. W. C. Davis
Haldeman Julius
Hall Caine
Hamilton Wright Mabie
Hans Christian Andersen
Harold Avery
Harold McGrath
Harriet Beecher Stowe
Harry Castlemon
Harry Coghill
Harry Houidini

Hayden Carruth
Helent Hunt Jackson
Helen Nicolay
Hendrik Conscience
Hendy David Thoreau
Henri Barbusse
Henrik Ibsen
Henry Adams
Henry Ford
Henry Frost
Henry James
Henry Jones Ford
Henry Seton Merriman
Henry W Longfellow
Herbert A. Giles
Herbert Carter
Herbert N. Casson
Herman Hesse
Hildegard G. Frey
Homer
Honore De Balzac
Horace B. Day
Horace Walpole
Horatio Alger Jr.
Howard Pyle
Howard R. Garis
Hugh Lofting
Hugh Walpole
Humphry Ward
Ian Maclaren
Inez Haynes Gillmore
Irving Bacheller
Isabel Cecilia Williams
Isabel Hornibrook
Israel Abrahams
Ivan Turgenev
J.G.Austin
J. Henri Fabre
J. M. Barrie
J. M. Walsh
J. Macdonald Oxley
J. R. Miller
J. S. Fletcher
J. S. Knowles
J. Storer Clouston
J. W. Duffield
Jack London
Jacob Abbott
James Allen
James Andrews
James Baldwin

James Branch Cabell
James DeMille
James Joyce
James Lane Allen
James Lane Allen
James Oliver Curwood
James Oppenheim
James Otis
James R. Driscoll
Jane Abbott
Jane Austen
Jane L. Stewart
Janet Aldridge
Jens Peter Jacobsen
Jerome K. Jerome
Jessie Graham Flower
John Buchan
John Burroughs
John Cournos
John F. Kennedy
John Gay
John Glasworthy
John Habberton
John Joy Bell
John Kendrick Bangs
John Milton
John Philip Sousa
John Taintor Foote
Jonas Lauritz Idemil Lie
Jonathan Swift
Joseph A. Altsheler
Joseph Carey
Joseph Conrad
Joseph E. Badger Jr
Joseph Hergesheimer
Joseph Jacobs
Jules Vernes
Julian Hawthrone
Julie A Lippmann
Justin Huntly McCarthy
Kakuzo Okakura
Karle Wilson Baker
Kate Chopin
Kenneth Grahame
Kenneth McGaffey
Kate Langley Bosher
Kate Langley Bosher
Katherine Cecil Thurston
Katherine Stokes
L. A. Abbot
L. T. Meade

L. Frank Baum
Latta Griswold
Laura Dent Crane
Laura Lee Hope
Laurence Housman
Lawrence Beasley
Leo Tolstoy
Leonid Andreyev
Lewis Carroll
Lewis Sperry Chafer
Lilian Bell
Lloyd Osbourne
Louis Hughes
Louis Joseph Vance
Louis Tracy
Louisa May Alcott
Lucy Fitch Perkins
Lucy Maud Montgomery
Luther Benson
Lydia Miller Middleton
Lyndon Orr
M. Corvus
M. H. Adams
Margaret E. Sangster
Margret Howth
Margaret Vandercook
Margaret W. Hungerford
Margret Penrose
Maria Edgeworth
Maria Thompson Daviess
Mariano Azuela
Marion Polk Angellotti
Mark Overton
Mark Twain
Mary Austin
Mary Catherine Crowley
Mary Cole
Mary Hastings Bradley
Mary Roberts Rinehart
Mary Rowlandson
M. Wollstonecraft Shelley
Maud Lindsay
Max Beerbohm
Myra Kelly
Nathaniel Hawthrone
Nicolo Machiavelli
O. F. Walton
Oscar Wilde

Owen Johnson
P.G. Wodehouse
Paul and Mabel Thorne
Paul G. Tomlinson
Paul Severing
Percy Brebner
Percy Keese Fitzhugh
Peter B. Kyne
Plato
Quincy Allen
R. Derby Holmes
R. L. Stevenson
R. S. Ball
Rabindranath Tagore
Rahul Alvares
Ralph Bonehill
Ralph Henry Barbour
Ralph Victor
Ralph Waldo Emmerson
Rene Descartes
Ray Cummings
Rex Beach
Rex E. Beach
Richard Harding Davis
Richard Jefferies
Richard Le Gallienne
Robert Barr
Robert Frost
Robert Gordon Anderson
Robert L. Drake
Robert Lansing
Robert Lynd
Robert Michael Ballantyne
Robert W. Chambers
Rosa Nouchette Carey
Rudyard Kipling
Saint Augustine
Samuel B. Allison
Samuel Hopkins Adams
Sarah Bernhardt
Sarah C. Hallowell
Selma Lagerlof
Sherwood Anderson
Sigmund Freud
Standish O'Grady
Stanley Weyman
Stella Benson
Stella M. Francis

Stephen Crane
Stewart Edward White
Stijn Streuvels
Swami Abhedananda
Swami Parmananda
T. S. Ackland
T. S. Arthur
The Princess Der Ling
Thomas A. Janvier
Thomas A Kempis
Thomas Anderton
Thomas Bailey Aldrich
Thomas Bulfinch
Thomas De Quincey
Thomas Dixon
Thomas H. Huxley
Thomas Hardy
Thomas More
Thornton W. Burgess
U. S. Grant
Upton Sinclair
Valentine Williams
Various Authors
Vaughan Kester
Victor Appleton
Victor G. Durham
Victoria Cross
Virginia Woolf
Wadsworth Camp
Walter Camp
Walter Scott
Washington Irving
Wilbur Lawton
Wilkie Collins
Willa Cather
Willard F. Baker
William Dean Howells
William le Queux
W. Makepeace Thackeray
William W. Walter
William Shakespeare
Winston Churchill
Yei Theodora Ozaki
Yogi Ramacharaka
Young E. Allison
Zane Grey